W9-BWZ-496

With Love From Spain, Melanie Martin

Praise for *The Diary of Melanie Martin:*

"Laugh-out-loud funny. . . . Weston's descriptions will have readers wanting to see Italy for themselves." —*School Library Journal*

"Weston clearly knows a ten-year-old's take on foreign customs. A humorous first novel. . . likeable, believable." —*Publishers Weekly*

"Charming. A right-as-rain take on the modern girl." —*Family Fun*

"Weston, advice columnist for *Girls' Life*, has her finger on that preadolescent girl pulse. . . . Captures the voice of the bright, excitable Melanie with ease, and the dynamics between the siblings are right on the money." —*The Bulletin*

"Fun, educational, poignant, humorous. Her diary, filled with great stories, keen observations, and quirky doodling, is a wonderful way to share the journey. Melanie finds more than statues and gelato on the other side of the ocean—she also finds herself." —*Children's Literature*

Praise for *Melanie Martin Goes Dutch:*

"A quirky kid pleaser." —*Vanity Fair*

"A breezy, fun, lighthearted read that quite naturally folds in contemporary issues. Her penchant for using words three times for emphasis [is] so, so, so right for the voice of the character. . . . Go, go, go, girl." —*Kirkus Reviews*

"While learning about Holland and seeing the sights, Melanie reads Anne Frank's diary and ponders the contrast between the magnitude of Anne's problems and her own. Achingly real . . . especially gratifying." —*Booklist*

"A favorite writer of preteen girls, Weston offers the latest installment in the ongoing adventures of a spunky young globetrotter." —*Yale Alumni Magazine*

"Great fun . . . makes you feel like you're visiting Amster-Amster-Dam-Dam-Dam too. A winner!" —*Discovery Girls*

With Love From Spain, Melanie Martin

BY

CARSOL WESTON

Alfred A. Knopf

New York

To my husband, Robert Ackerman,
and to three Spanish *caballeros*—
Juan, Pipo, Andreu

THIS IS A BORZOI BOOK PUBLISHED BY ALFRED A. KNOPF

www.randomhouse.com/kids

Library of Congress Cataloging-in-Publication Data
Weston, Carol.
With love from Spain, Melanie Martin / by Carol Weston.
p. cm.
SUMMARY: While spending spring break in Spain with her family, eleven-year-old Melanie keeps a diary of her experiences improving her Spanish, struggling with her little brother, meeting her mother's former boyfriend, and falling in love with his son.

ISBN 0-375-82646-7 (trade) — ISBN 0-375-92646-1 (lib. bdg.)
[1. Love—Fiction. 2. Voyages and travels—Fiction. 3. Family life—Fiction. 4. Spanish language—Fiction. 5. Diaries—Fiction. 6. Spain—Fiction.] I. Title.
PZ7.W526285Wi2004
[Fic]—dc21 2003047628

Printed in the United States of America
January 2004
10 9 8 7 6 5 4 3 2 1
First Edition

Spain
Portugal
Bilbao
Pamplona
Valladolid
Zaragoza
Barcelona
Segovia
Madrid
Toledo
Valencia
Balearic
Islands
Cordoba
Seville
Granada

March 16

on board and on vacation

Dear Diary,

Four more hours till we land in SPAIN!

If I didn't have my seat belt on, I'd be jumping UP and down.

We have been waiting waiting waiting for spring break and it's finally here! NO early-morning wake-ups, NO pop quizzes, and NO homework—for two weeks anyway.

Since Dad had to go to Madrid on business, Mom used frequent-flyer miles so we could all tag along.

Today they picked us up after school, and we went straight to the airport.

I'm excited about this trip because I speak Spanish—

hablo español (Ah Blow S Pon Yole). Not fluently or anything, but I know how to count. One is *uno* (Oo No), two is *dos* (Dose), and three is *tres* (Trace). I can also say hi, which is *hola* (Oh La), and lots of other words.

I hope I meet a nice Spanish girl so I can learn more.

Right now I'm in seat 22 next to Matt the Brat. He asked me, "Are the street signs in Spain in Spanish?"

"Duh," I said, and made a how-stupid-can-you-get face.

"Wrong!" He laughed. "They're in sign language!"

Believe it or not, that joke was better than some of his other second-grade humor. In the taxi, for instance, Matt said, "What goes ha-ha-ha-ha-splat?" I said, "What?" and he said, "A man laughing his head off."

Well, that was so lame that I said, "You came out funny. That's why Mom and Dad stopped having kids after they had you."

He said, "*You* came out funny. That's why Mom and Dad had me."

Fortunately, Matt is now asleep. His eyes are closed and his mouth is open. Mom and Dad told us to try to sleep because when we arrive, it will be morning of a brand-new day—ready or not.

Problem is, I'm not sleepy. Something is bothering me.

All of us are excited about this vacation, but Mom might be too excited.

An old friend of hers is picking us up at the airport.

And not just any old friend. An old *boy*friend!

And not just any old boyfriend. A "serious" old boyfriend.

His name is Antonio (On Toe Knee Oh).

All I know about him is that he smokes—which is disgusting. And he speaks English but makes mistakes. And he has a kid. And his last name is Ramón (Rah Moan).

How could Mom have gone out with someone who can't speak English without making mistakes? And who smokes??

Last weekend Mom showed me ancient photos of them together. In one, they were holding hands at a zoo. In another, they had their arms around each other in front of a castle.

Mom's friend Lori was visiting, and she and Mom started looking at scrapbooks and giggling as if they were still college roommates.

"I can't believe you and Antonio have started e-mailing!" Lori said.

"I can't believe I'm about to see him after all these years!" Mom answered.

"That's my fantasy," Lori said. "To see an old boyfriend when I'm with my husband and kids. No, wait! I think my fantasy is to see an old boyfriend when I'm all by myself!" Lori laughed and laughed. It made me feel w-e-i-r-d. "Think he's still tall, dark, and handsome?"

"Who knows?" Mom answered.

"Well, get your beauty sleep on the plane," Lori said as she was leaving. "And give Antonio a big kiss for me."

Get this: Mom asked, "How big?" and they both giggled!

I wonder if Mom and Antonio ever did kiss.

Is that a dumb thing to wonder? Obviously, they must have.

I was tempted to say something to Mom, but I didn't want her to think I was eavesdropping.

Which I wasn't. I was in the kitchen finding common denominators of fractions and I accidentally overheard their conversation.

I have to say, Mom has been acting strange all week.

On Monday, she bought a lip gloss and a pink scarf. On Tuesday, she got a haircut even though her hair looked perfectly fine. On Wednesday, she had a manicure. (Mom hardly ever gets her nails done.) Yesterday, she bought a blouse and a pair of pants.

I called Cecily to tell her about Mom's giggling and shopping and makeover. Cecily pointed out that she and I like giggling and shopping and makeovers and said, "Don't worry." She always tells me not to worry. But I always end up worrying.

I thought about asking Dad if he's noticed anything suspicious. I even considered warning him that Mom is trying to look good for her ex Spanish Sweetheart.

Would that be betraying Mom?

Maybe I am making too big a deal of this.

Maybe not!

By the way, for my birthday, I got a new diary—you!—which I saved for this plane ride. But now I'm going to put you away and wrap the airplane blanket around myself (and Hedgie) so we can try to fall asleep.

I was going to bring a different stuffed animal and leave Hedgehog safe at home. But I couldn't bear to. (Or hedgehog to, get it?) Matt did leave DogDog behind. He said he couldn't stand it if DogDog got lost again like on our last trip. So he brought his penguin, Flappy Happy. It is black and white with a yellow beak and trusting eyes.

Good night, or as they say in Spain, Good nights.

Buenas noches (Bway Nahs No Chase)—

March 17
STILL on board

Dear Diary,

Instead of getting a good night's sleep, I got a bad night's nap. It's time to get up, though, because it's already morning here, and after this long flight, we have to take a short flight so we can meet You Know Who.

When we all get off this plane,
We will be in Madrid, Spain.
When our travels reach an end,
Mom will see her old BOYFRIEND.

Mom said to get our shoes on and be ready to run.

Here's how Matt ties his shoes: He makes two jumbo loops—which he calls bunny ears—crosses them while poking out the tip of his tongue, tucks one loop inside the other, and pulls.

Here's how I tie my shoes: the normal way.

Sometimes I wonder if Matt will be immature his whole life long. He even got Dad in trouble.

What happened was, Mom said that flight attendants used to be called stewardesses and that "stewardesses" is the longest word you can type with just your left hand. Matt asked, "In Spanish too?" Mom said, "No, in Spanish, the word is *azafatas*." Well, instead of hearing Ah Sa Fot Ahs, Matt heard a really bad phrase that Mom would never say about a person's behind.

He started laughing and said, "Some flight attendants have *azafatas*!"

Mom looked unamused. But Dad smiled a teeny-weeny bit and added, "No ifs, ands, or butts."

That got Mom mad. She said, "Honey, can't you at least *try* to set a good example?"

Dad actually seemed torn! Maybe parents sometimes feel like acting like kids instead of role models for kids?

Uh-oh, the seat belt sign went off, and everyone is standing up.

Except me. I'm going to keep writing until the line starts moving.

It started moving!

Good mornings or

Buenos días (Bway Nohs Dee Ahs)—

Melanie on the Move

SAME DAY

smaller plane

Dear Diary,

One thing I've noticed: Airports are full of happy hellos and weepy goodbyes. I never cry in airports because when I go places, I go with my family, so there's no reason to get all emotional. When Dad has to fly somewhere on business, we don't have sad farewell scenes either, because before we know it, he comes back home to New York.

We are now flying from Madrid to Valencia. Dad said Valencia is Spain's third-largest city and that lots of oranges and clementines come from Valencia. (I eat clementines by the box!)

Mom says Spaniards pronounce some v's almost like b's and some c's and z's in a lisping way. In Castillian Spanish, Valencia is Ba Lenth E Ah. "You can often tell where people are from by how they talk."

"Like, if a person says, 'Pahk the cah,' he might be from Boston?" I asked.

"Yes," Mom said.

"And if he says, 'Howdy, y'all,' he might be from Texas?" Matt added.

"Yes," Mom said.

"Do people in Valencia, Barcelona, Madrid, and Seville have different accents?" We'll be visiting those cities, so I thought that was a good question.

Mom nodded, but she was barely paying attention. She was brushing her hair.

Is Antonio at the airport brushing his hair?

Does he still have hair?

Maybe he's gone bald. And gotten unhandsome.

Matt went to the bathroom, and I decided that instead of worrying, I'd confront Mom. So I asked, "Mom, do you still have feelings for that Spanish guy?"

I was sure she'd say, "Of course not—don't be silly."

But she didn't. She said, "Pumpkin, if you ever really care about someone, you always have some feelings tucked away in a little corner of your heart."

What?!

I probably looked like I was going to faint, and I was about to say that hearts don't even have corners, but Mom added, "Sweet pea, I love Daddy! But Antonio and I have a sort of frozen friendship. Just because he and I broke up doesn't mean I threw away all the old photos or old memories. My junior year abroad was a big part of my life, and Antonio and his family were a big part of that year."

"But—" I started to say. But I didn't have an end to the sentence.

Mom continued, "Lives have chapters, just like books. When you read a book, you don't tear out the chapters you've already read, right?"

"I guess not. . . ." I tried to picture Mom living her life before I was born. It was totally impossible.

"Oh, Mel, it's natural that I'm curious to see Antonio again, but Daddy is my Number One Man. My *Número Uno*" (Noo Mare Oh Ooo No).

Dad, meanwhile, was fast asleep with his shoulders drooped and his head slumped forward and his lips puffed out. "We're about to land," Mom told him, but he just grunted twice.

I Know my father needs his rest,
But with his chin upon his chest,
He really does not look his best.

I'm just glad Mom didn't marry Antonionionio (as Matt calls him). And that Dad didn't marry that Sophia lady we bumped into last year at the Colosseum.

What worries me is this: We bumped into Sophia by accident; we're bumping into Antonio on purpose.

Matt came back and said, "You know what you are when you're in the bathroom?"

"What?" I asked.

"European! You're a-peein'! Get it?"

"Euromoron! You're a moron! Get it?" I replied.

Mom ignored us and asked, "How do I look?"

I was tempted to say, "Like a middle-aged married mother," but I said, "Fine." Mom always looks fine—for an M.M.M. Which is good, because it's embarrassing enough that she teaches art at my school. It would be way worse if she dressed weird or had poor personal hygiene.

She is now gazing out the window and adjusting her pink scarf.

The *azafata* said to put up my tray table, so I better put you away.

We're about to see Spain— Yippee!!

We're about to see Antonio—Yipes!!

Adiós (Odd E Ose)

or BYE,

Melanie

1ST day in España (S Pon Ya) or Spain

in Antonio's Car

Dear Diary,

The plane landed and Mom headed straight for the exit while Dad had to deal with our carry-ons in the overhead bin. Poor Dad. He's the family pack mule. I think Mom wanted to have a moment alone with *Señor* (Say Nyor) Smoker, but I bounded after her.

Dad did not hire
A private eye.
So just call me—
Melanie the Spy.

At the airport, a man came right up to Mom. He wasn't running with his arms out or anything, but he kissed her on both cheeks and said, "Miranda!" which he pronounced Me Ron Dah. Then he checked her out and said, "*¡Estás igual!*" (S Tahs E Gwahl), which means "You look the same."

"You too!" Mom said. "You haven't changed a bit!" This had to be a total lie because trust me, he did *not* look like a college student!

He laughed and patted his stomach. "I have more weight now—but I am good cook! I have made lunch for your family."

I took "family" as my cue to remind Mom that she wasn't exactly here on junior year abroad.

"*Hola,*" I said.

"*¡Hola!*" Antonio said, and smiled. "*¿Hablas español?*" (Ah Blahs S Pon Yole).

I knew that meant "Do you speak Spanish?" so I said, "*Sí, un poquito*" (See Oon Poe Key Toe), which means "Yes, a little bit."

He said, "I am Antonio," and leaned over and kissed me.

I answered, "I am Melanie." Matt showed up, so I added, "This is Matt. *Tiene siete años*" (Tyeh Nay Syeh Tay On Nyose). That means "He is seven."

I was glad I remembered that in Spanish, you don't say, "He *is* seven," you say, "He *has* seven years." I think I sounded proud of myself and I hoped Antonio realized that I was proud of saying a Spanish sentence—not of having an American brother!

Dad appeared with our carry-on baggage. "I'm Marc. Very nice to meet you."

"Equally." They shook hands. Mom's friend Lori had said that Antonio was "tall, dark, and handsome," but Dad is taller and I think handsomer. Antonio said, "Welcome to Spain," but he pronounced it "S Pain," which I hoped wasn't a bad sign.

The grown-ups kept talking, and I figured we were off to a pretty good start. But what had I expected? A duel?

Antonio said, "I hope you will enjoy *Las Fallas*" (Las Fie Yahs).

Mom's excuse for making us visit her old flame (as Dad calls him) is that Valencia has its annual festival, *Las Fallas* or The Bonfires, during our spring break. It's a big *fiesta* (Fee S Tah) or party with firecrackers, fireworks, and fires.

It sounds kind of kooky, but groups of Spaniards spend a whole entire year building giant wood and papier-mâché structures called *fallas*. Around 350 of them! They put them on the streets, and for five days, everybody admires them. Judges give out prizes and also pick part of one *falla* to be put in a museum. Then on March 19—this Monday—the rest get burned to the ground.

We waited for our bags, and Antonio said he was going to take us to the *Mascletà* (Mahs Clay Ta), which is a firecracker celebration. While the grown-ups talked, I found a luggage cart, Matt climbed in, and I took him on an airport tour. He was Mr. Happy Boy!

Fortunately, every one of our bags arrived (yay!), so we put them in Antonio's car. It has a white oval bumper sticker with a black letter E for *España*. Dad told Mom to sit up front with Antonio, which surprised me. Shouldn't Dad make sure they don't start liking each other again?

Maybe Dad was too exhausted to be jealous because the second he sat down in the backseat, he passed out.

Matt too. Does Dad have any idea how dumb he looks when he's asleep? This time his head is tilted back and his mouth is wide open. I wonder if I should close it. I hope Antonio doesn't look in the rearview mirror. So far he hasn't. He is too busy driving and looking at Me Ron Dah. They are talking a mile a minute in Spanish and I don't understand a single solitary word.

Antonionio is now parking the car. We're here! But where?

Hasta luego (Ah Sta Loo Way Go)

or See you later,

Melanie in Mystery

@ 5:00 p.m.
in a hammock

Dear Diary,

I COULD NOT BELIEVE MY EARS!

No one could have slept through what we heard today.

Antonio parked, I poked Matt and Dad awake, and we all walked to a square packed with people. We inched our way toward the middle of the mob. Antonio said to cover our ears because at 2:00 P.M. sharp, firecrackers were going to go off for several minutes, and we would not just hear them—we would *feel* them in our stomachs and under our feet.

I braced myself and wondered, Is this town full of pyromaniacs? (I just learned that word. It means people who want to set fires.)

At 2:00, everybody stopped talking. They were waiting for the noise, but there was no noise. There was a delay. So you know what the smooshed people did? They whistled! When American audiences are unhappy, they boo or maybe hiss, but when Spaniards are unhappy, they whistle.

Well, the whistling didn't last long because at about 2:01, there was a thundering drumroll that went on and on and on. Like a zillion sticks of dynamite.

KABOOM BOOM!

BOOM BOOM BOOM!

Matt decided then and there that he LOVED Spain.

Little boys
Love loud noise
Even more than
They love toys.

Dad looked at me as if to say, "Is this supposed to be fun?" and I shrugged as if to answer, "Don't ask me." It *is* strange! Close your eyes, and it was a war zone. Open them, and it was a citywide block party—a party that goes on for almost three weeks.

When the explosions stopped, Antonio looked at Mom. She smiled a half smile. He said, "I do not like the *Mascletà*, but I wanted you to have the experience."

"Experience" in Spanish is *experiencia* (X Pair E N C Ah). Mom said some long words are similar in English and Spanish. "Adventure" is *aventura* (Ah Ben Too Ra). "Television" is *televisión* (Tay Lay V Syon). "Clementine" is *clementina* (Clem N T Na). Mom said it's fun to say English words with a Spanish accent and hope for the best. Some English words are spelled the same in Spanish, like "patio," "piano," "radio," and "mosquito."

We waded through the crowd until we got back to

Antonio's car. He drove us to his home outside Valencia and asked, "Are you angry?"

Even though I hadn't 100% loved getting my eardrums shattered, I wasn't angry, so I said, "No."

Mom looked surprised. "You aren't *hungry*?"

Oh! Hungry!! Mom obviously understands the whole accent thing better than we do.

I said, "I *am* hungry," and Matt added, "I am *starving*."

Spaniards eat lunch really late—at 2:00 or 3:00 instead of 12:00 or 1:00!

Antonio had prepared *paella valenciana* (Pie Ay Ya Ba Len C Ah Na). It is a famous Spanish dish made with rice and saffron. Saffron is a spice that comes from dried insides of crocus flowers. You need a lot of flowers to get a little saffron, so it costs a lot. It is orange-red and turns rice yummy yellow. Antonio's paella also had peas, beans, peppers, cut-up chicken, and, I hate to write this but . . . rabbit.

He used a round shallow two-handled pan and put in ingredients he had already chopped up. It bubbled and cooked and we waited and waited and waited.

It smelled soooo good!

Matt asked, "Is it really spicy?" but Mom said that Mexican food is sometimes spicy, not Spanish food.

Matt said, "Knock knock."

Mom said, "Who's there?"

Matt said, "Sombrero."

I said, "Sombrero who?" and Matt started singing, "Som brere ohhhver the rainbow—" until I made him stop.

Anyway, here's how the paella tasted: scrumptious or *rico* (Rrree Co). Actually, I ate only the rice and chicken—not the rabbit. I'm not an adventurous eater, and besides, I kept thinking about Cecily's pet rabbit, Honey Bunny. So I picked out all the rabbit pieces and pushed them to one side of my plate. Since I didn't even want to look at them, I offered them to Dad. He said, "Sure," and transferred them onto his plate. (It's helpful that he's a B.P.—a Big Pig!)

The grown-ups also had Spanish champagne called *cava* (Ca Ba) and giant shrimp appetizers called *langostinos* (Lang Oh Steen Ohs). Mom beamed and said everything was *delicioso* (Day Lee Syoh So). "Antonio, do you always eat this well?"

He smiled. "No. Only on special occasions."

I hope Dad is paying attention to how special it is for Antonio and Mom to see each other again!

I asked Mom where Antonio's wife was and Mom whispered, "They recently separated, remember?" She added, "That's another word that's almost the same in Spanish—*separado*" (Say Par Odd Oh).

Well, I did *not* remember, and who wants to learn that word?!

Right now the grown-ups are drinking coffee and eating almond candy called *turrón* (Two Rrrohn). I didn't like it. Antonio is also smoking (yuck!) and making Mom and Dad laugh some more. Matt whispered, "He doesn't seem so serious."

"What do you mean?" I asked.

"You said he was a serious boyfriend," Matt said.

"A serious boyfriend doesn't mean the *person* is serious, Doo-doo Head! It means the *relationship* is serious!" (Sometimes Matt is not the brightest crayon in the box.)

Matt looked confused, but I was too jet-lagged to explain. Besides, Mom is making us both take a nap. I'm going to take my *siesta* (See S Ta) right here in this hammock in Antonio's backyard. We need to sleep because Antonio has big plans for us tonight.

Sleepily—

Late Late Late

Antonio's brother's apartment

Dear Diary,

We are staying in the apartment of Antonio's brother. His name is Angel, which, I'm sorry to say, is pronounced On Hell. Angel is lending it to us because he and Mom used to be friends, and he always goes away during the festival because he doesn't like noise and crowds.

Valencia *is* noisy and crowded right now!

We walked around the old part of town until my legs practically fell off. It's good that they didn't fall off or they would have gotten stepped on by thousands of people. There was a big parade or procession—*procesión* (Pro Sess C Yohn)—of dressed-up Valencians: men and boys in fancy embroidered vests with shiny brass buttons, and women and girls in puffy dresses with lacy veils and red-and-yellow sashes. They were all wearing traditional Spanish clothes, and they looked like princes and princesses. Or grooms and brides. Or life-size dolls.

The celebration was called *Ofrenda de Flores* (Oh Friend Da Day Floor S) or Offering of Flowers. A big thick line of people was carrying piles of bouquets through the town up to a cathedral, where they stacked them row upon row against the church wall.

It was beautiful!

Dad was walking with Matt and me, and Mom and Antonio were walking a few steps ahead. A giant amber moon was lighting up everything—the night-time parade, ancient stone walls, octagonal bell tower, and even Mom and Antonio.

All of a sudden, I *could* picture the two of them as a couple! And I *could* picture Mom as a regular woman before I came along and turned her into a mom.

It made me dizzy.

I reached for Dad's hand and said, "I'm too tired to keep going." Well, we tried to leave, but there were so many people, we could barely budge, let alone make a fast exit.

Spaniards are night owls! We could still even hear a few faraway firecrackers. (That's an alliteration.) POP POP POP (So is that.)

Matt said *he* was falling-down drop-dead tired too, and Dad lifted him onto his shoulders. Sometimes I wish Dad could still carry me.

We finally got out, and Antonio drove us back here.

Mom thanked Antonio for a wonderful day. It *was* a wonderful day. But it was one of the longest days in my whole eleven-year life. The last time I was in a bed with sheets and a pillow was in New York, so it was a *double* day, and I am exhaust.

Did I just write "I am exhaust"? I am not exhaust!! I am *exhausted*!!

Tomorrow we are meeting Antonio's kid and going to a bullfight. I told Antonio that I hope he got us bad seats because I don't want to sit up close. He laughed even though I wasn't trying to be funny.

It won't be very dark when I turn off the bedside lamp because moonlight is streaming in through the window.

Pleasant dreams and sleep tight—
Melanie in the Moonlight

March 18
Noonish

Dear Diary,

I can't believe that the day before yesterday was just an ordinary school day. Fifth-grade Spanish class with Cecily, Christopher, Norbert, and *Señora* (Say Nyor Ah) Barrios seems like forever ago!

I like how trips make time S-T-R-E-T-C-H. First you look forward to a trip. Then you enjoy it.

Then you look back on it. If you ask me what I did last summer, for instance, a lot of it is a big blur. But if you ask about our week bicycling around Amsterdam, I could tell you all about it.

Today Matt and I slept until noon—dawn in Manhattan. We'd still be snoozing, except Mom woke us up, saying, "Hop up, kiddos! I now pronounce you good as new. You're officially on Spanish time!"

I would have rolled my eyes except that just opening them was enough of a challenge.

Mom and Dad are drinking coffee or *café* (Calf Ay). Dad always jokes that coffee is an important part of a balanced breakfast. They were also listening to classical music (*música* or Moo Z Ca) by a dead Spanish guy named Rodrigo (Road Ree Go).

While we were having breakfast, Matt said, "I bet I can make you say black."

I said, "I bet you can't."

"What are the colors of the American flag?"

"Red, white, and blue."

"What are the colors of the Spanish flag?"

"Red and yellow."

"What color is grass?"

"Green."

"I told you I could make you say green!"

"You said black!"

"Ha ha! And you just said it!"

What an A.L.B.—Annoying Little Brother! I can't believe I fell for that!!

After our noon breakfast, Matt made me play Towel Bullfight. I hold up a towel and flap it in the air. He gets down on all fours, snorts, points his pointer fingers out from his forehead, and charges. Then I snap the towel away and flap it on the other side, and he charges again. He looks demented, but he loves it.

Mom said we should dress nicely because going to a bullfight here is like going to the theater at home—you shouldn't just show up in jeans.

How can a bullfight be like theater? And what *will* it be like?

Gotta go! Antonio and his kid are ringing the doorbell.

Hasta pronto (Ah Sta Pron Toe)

or See You Soon,

Mellie

same day (even though that doesn't seem possible)

on a [bench] outside the [bullring] (bullring)

Dear Diary,

Antonio's kid is twelve and a half! He's a boy! And he's cute!

His name is Miguel.

He has brown hair and brown eyes and a nice accent and a nice smile.

And he speaks English—pretty well, anyway.

Here's how he says my name: May Lah Nee.

Here's how I say his: Meeg L. (You don't pronouce the U in Miguel, same as you don't pronounce the U in guitar.)

When Antonio introduced us, Miguel looked right at me and said, "*Encantado*" (N Con Todd Oh), which means "Enchanted." Then he kissed me on both cheeks!

I thought I would keel over. But I didn't. I just started smiling and couldn't stop.

We all got into Antonio's car—this time Dad sat up front—and it was squooshy but I didn't mind because I was squooshed against Miguel.

The plan was for them to show us around and then for just us four to go to the bullfight.

Miguel asked me if I like Spain and I said, "*Sí sí sí.*"

Antonio drove us to a place called the City of Arts and Sciences. A "brilliant architect" named Calatrava (Cahl Ah Tra Va) built it. He is from Valencia and has bushy eyebrows. The buildings are white and space-age-y. One looks like the skeleton of a whale and another like a giant eyeball. Mom said Calatrava designed a section of an art museum in Milwaukee. It has wings that flap and it looks like it's about to take off.

We took a walk by a row of palm trees growing *inside* a glass building. We also saw a big pendulum and a twisty floor-to-ceiling model of DNA.

Dad likes how the science museum was a Please Touch (not a Don't Touch) museum.

Mom likes how Valencia has really ancient buildings, really modern buildings, and lots of bridges.

I like Miguel.

This trip is going very well.
I met a cute boy named Miguel.

He bought popcorn. In Spanish, popcorn is *palomitas* (Pa Low Me Tahs), which means little doves. Maybe because if you throw them in the air, they flutter? Miguel kept offering me little doves and I kept saying *gracias* (Grah Sea Ahs), which means thank you. Once our fingertips sort of met inside the popcorn bag. I pulled mine away and could feel myself blushing.

Whenever I share popcorn with Matt, we always get into a fight because one of us accuses the other of eating too fast—gobbling the popcorn up by the handful instead of a few at a time. Or else we agree to eat the white ones first and *then* the yellow ones, but one of us forgets and does it wrong.

Miguel and I did not argue at all.

Even though it was sunny, there was a cool breeze and I suddenly got goose bumps. Mom said that goose bumps in Spanish are called chicken skin or *piel de gallina* (Pyel Day Guy Ye Na). Matt thought "chicken skin" sounded funny, and Miguel and Antonio thought "goose bumps" sounded funny, so everyone was laughing. Except me. I didn't like that the topic of conversation was my sticking-up arm hairs.

I was rubbing my arms trying to make the goose bumps go away (can you *make* goose bumps go away?) when Miguel offered me his sweater. I said, "No, it's okay," but he gently insisted. He said, "You have cold." I was about to say, "I don't have a cold." But I remembered that in Spanish, instead of saying, "You *are* cold," you say, "You *have* cold" or *Tienes frío* (Tyeh Ness Free Oh).

I said, "*Un poco*" (Oon Poe Coe), which means "a little." That's when he took off his sweater and draped it around me!

Isn't that romantic??!!

No boy in America has ever shared his sweater with me!

I said, "*Gracias*," and smiled. The sweater was big on me but it felt nice and warm. We kept walking and I said, "These buildings are cool."

"You should see them lighted at night, May Lah Nee."

I couldn't tell if he was making conversation—or halfway asking me out?!

Antonio said, "*¿Tomamos algo?*" (Toe Mom Ose Ahl Go). Even though it is just two words in Spanish, Mom translated them as, "Shall we go get something to eat and drink?"

I said, "*Sí,*" and we squooshed back into the car. This time Freckle-Face Matt got in between Miguel and me. I don't know if Matt was being bratty on purpose or by accident, but I wished we could switch places.

We were driving along and suddenly we heard what sounded like an earthquake.

"What's that?" I asked. "*¿Qué es?*" (K S).

"*La Mascletà,*" Miguel said. "It is two o'clock." He checked his watch.

"I thought that was yesterday."

"It is every day of *Las Fallas*," he explained. "It starts March first and happens at midday until March nineteenth."

"That's *un poco loco*—a little crazy." I felt good about making a rhyme in Spanish, but I hoped I hadn't offended Miguel. He repeated "*un poco loco*" and laughed. His eyes twinkled and I tried to make mine twinkle back. (Can you *make* your eyes twinkle?)

Well, instead of having a sit-down two-course big-deal lunch, we went bar-hopping. That may sound inappropriate for kids, but it's what Spanish families sometimes do. Antonio took us into a bar and ordered beer for the grown-ups and plates of ham-and-potato omelette for everybody to share.

Not exactly my Dream Meal.

I probably wouldn't have tried any of it, but Miguel said, "Spain is famous for its delicious ham."

I said, "*¿Delicioso?*" and he said, "Try," so I did.

"You like?" he asked. I wanted to say, "I like *you*!" but I just said, "*¡Sí!*"

He said, "Ham in Spanish is *jamón*" (Hhhahm Own).

Now that I think about it, I guess our conversation wasn't the height of romance, but somehow it felt like we were saying more.

I repeated, "*Jamón*," and said, "You are a good teacher."

He said, "You are good student."

Were we being friendly? Or were we flirting??

I wasn't sure—I'm new at this!

Miguel asked, "You have tried *tortilla*?" (Tor T Ya). I wanted to say, "No, but that's okay." *Tortilla* means omelette, and Spanish omelettes are not served hot; they come room temperature and stuffed with potatoes. Miguel said it is a specialty and he speared a cube of *tortilla* with a toothpick and handed it to me. If Matt had offered me a *tortilla* kebab, I probably would have said, "Gross!" But since it was Miguel at the other end of the toothpick, I said, "*Gracias*," and ate it in one bite.

It was better than I expected.

Everything was. Does food taste better when you're happy?

We went to a second bar, and Antonio ordered barnacles. Hungry or happy or not, there was no way I was going to eat squishy squiggly barnacle insides—no matter who offered them. Antonio, Miguel, Mom, and Dad raved about them. Miguel said they are a delicacy and that fishermen scrape them off rocks while watching out for huge waves.

Dad said they taste like the sea. Well, a huge wave once knocked me over, and the sea is not a flavor I want to taste again. So I just ate bread.

"You like bullfights?" Miguel asked.

"*No sé*" (No Say), I said, which means I don't know. I told him I'd never seen one.

"Later you tell me your impression, okay, May Lah Nee?"

I love how he says May Lah Nee.

Our names sound nice together too: Miguel and Melanie. May Lah Nee and Meeg L.

We Martins are the 4-M family (Melanie, Matt, Miranda, and Marc), and in the back back back of my mind, I've always wondered if I might someday marry someone named Max or Michael or Mitch or...........?!

Never mind! My imagination is totally out of control!!

Miguel said, "Keep the sweater for now. I don't want you to have cold."

I thought:

What could be sweeter
Than wearing your sweater?

After lunch, Antonio handed Dad four bullfight tickets, and Dad handed him a bunch of euros, which is money. The Spanish used to pay with *pesetas* (Pay Say Tahs), but now people use euros all around Europe.

Antonio and Miguel are going to meet us for dinner. I wish it were dinnertime!

Love,
May Lah Nee

4:45 P.M.

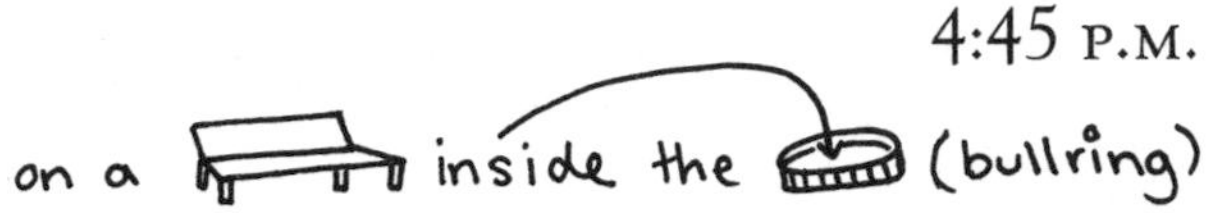

Dear Diary,

In New York, when we go to musicals, up close is better than far back. But if you're *too* up close, you can end up seeing all the spit that spurts out of the singers' mouths, and it can be gross.

In a bullring, if you're too up close, it could be way grosser. You'd smell the hairy bulls and see their sweat and cuts and blood and guts (a disgusting almost poem).

Matt said this place reminds him of *The Story of Ferdinand*, the book about the nice bull.

It reminds me of a Yankee game. But while a baseball field is a diamond, and a football field is a rectangle, a bullring is a circle—and not a circle of life like in *The Lion King*. A circle of death!

"For Halloween," Matt just said, "I'm going to be a bullfighter."

"Or you could be a dork. Then you wouldn't need a costume."

He looked kind of hurt and I felt kind of bad. Mean things sometimes pop out even when we're getting along. "Kidding," I said. "You can be a bullfighter. Or even a bull! You'd be a great bull. You've been practicing!"

"Marc, I don't see any other children here," Mom said. "Not many women either. I hope this is a good idea." She said she's never seen a bullfight because Antonio thought they were cruel and barbaric.

"Oh pleeeease," Dad said.

"Is this going to be fun?" I asked.

"Some consider it an art form," Mom said.

"Spain has had bullfights for centuries," Dad added. "This might be interesting, exciting, possibly even beautiful. But no, Melleroo, not necessarily fun."

A brass band just started playing, and bullfighters, or *toreros* (Tore Air Ohs), are entering the ring. Uh-oh, the bullfight is about to begin!

Anxiously yours,

@ 6:00 p.m.

Dear Diary,

I expected *one* bull to bite the dust. But every bull-fight has *six* different bulls and *three* different matadors.

I am in Spain at a bullfight.
I have to say, it's quite a sight.
I never thought six bulls would die.
It sort of makes me want to cry.

When the first bull, or *toro* (Tore Oh), came into the ring, I wanted to name him Bullwinkle, and Matt wanted to name him Buddy. We started arguing, and Dad said, "Kids, do yourselves a favor and don't name him at all. He'll be dead before you know it."

And he was! ☹

Matt and I felt awful when the bull rolled over, his four dusty little hooves sticking up in the air.

Men tied him up by his horns, and mules dragged him off, and out came Bull #2, puffing and pawing and snorting and stomping.

I said, "I don't want to see this bull get hurt."

Dad said, "Then, cupcake, you came to the wrong

place." He patted my knee and said I could cover my eyes.

"Do the bulls ever win?" Matt asked. "Or is it a setup?"

"An upsetting setup," I said.

"How could it be a setup?" Dad said. "It's man versus beast, or once in a while, woman versus beast."

"I know what I *don't* want to be when I grow up," Matt said. "A bullfighter!"

"Me neither."

To fight a bull
Takes lots of guts.
You'd have to be
A little nuts.

I took a quick peek at Bull #2. BIG mistake! Six harpoons were sticking out of the hump in his back. "He looks like a porcupine!" I announced. "He's bleeding! Can we leave?"

Dad reminded me that he asked weeks ago if I wanted to go, and I said yes, so long as we didn't have to sit up close.

Well, the reason I said yes was not because I wanted to *see* a bullfight. It was because for the rest of my life,

I wanted to be able to *say* that I had seen a bullfight! There's a difference!

I am now writing in you instead of looking at what's happening to Porcupine Bull.

The matador's big moment of glory
Is, for the bull, an end that is gory.

Matt just said, "Mellie, stop writing for a sec and look at Bull Number Three. He really is like Ferdinand!"

You know what? Matt's right! Bull #3 isn't stomping or charging; he's strolling around minding his own business.

"This time, I'm rooting for the bull," Matt said.

"I don't know who to root for," I said.

"Whom," Mom mumbled.

Well, the officials must have decided that this bull is a bore because other bulls just entered the ring and lured Sweetie Pie out.

Matt and I cheered. (We were the only ones, though.)

Now a giant non-Ferdinandy substitute bull is racing in, ready for action.

Matt said, "*Hola*" to a white-haired man sitting next

to us, and now Mom and the Spanish Grandpa Guy are babbling away. He said he was enchanted to meet me and asked, "*¿Te gusta España?*" (Tay Goose Ta S Pon Ya), which means, "Do you like Spain?"

I said, "*Sí*, but not bullfights."

He laughed and said, "You will let me explain?" (Mom translated.)

I said, "*Sí*."

Grandpa Guy said, "First, you see two *picadores* (Peek A Door Ays) on horseback. Their job is to poke the bull with long lances and make him mad."

"I hate the pokador part," Matt whispered. (He said "pokador.")

"Me too. I feel sorry for the bull and the horses." I stuck out my lower lip, and Matt made a matching face.

Grandpa Guy said, "Next, you see three *bandilleros* (Bon D Yair Ohs) with red-and-yellow-ribboned harpoons. Their job is to stab the bull and slow him down."

"It's so not fair!" I whispered to Matt. "It's not one-on-one. It's one bull and a bunch of bullies!"

"Yeah, but, Mel, the bull is by far the scariest thing out there! Look at the horns on him!"

"Good points," I said, but Matt didn't get it.

Grandpa Guy said, "Finally, you see the matador. You know his job, yes?"

In case we didn't, Mom informed us that *matador* (Matt Adore) comes from the verb *matar* (Matt R), which means kill.

I used Dad's opera glasses to check the killer out. Here's how he's dressed: in pink socks and bright-bright tight-tight golden pants that stop below his knees and an embroidered golden jacket with shiny shoulder pads. The pants are really really really tight because if they were baggy, the bull's needle-sharp horns could get caught in them. He also has on dainty slippers and a black cap with Mouseketeer ears. Grandpa Guy said the outfit is called a suit of lights. His cape is red, but bulls care about flapping, *not* color. Bulls are color-blind!!

Mom pointed out the matador's photo in our program. "He's twenty. Isn't he handsome?"

Since when did Mom start noticing handsome guys? Or has she always?

Does she have a thing for Spanish men?

Do I?!

Matt asked, “Do bullfighters make a lot of money?”

Mom said, “A few become rich and famous, like athletes and pop stars.”

Matt asked Grandpa Guy if he’d ever seen a bullfighter get killed. Turns out this matador had a famous father who died in the ring! You’d think a son would not follow a dad’s footsteps into a bullring, but in Spain, lots of little boys dream of becoming bullfighters.

Dad told Grandpa Guy he was reading a book called *Death in the Afternoon* by an American named Hemingway. Grandpa Guy’s eyes lit up. He said Hemingway is popular in Spain because he makes people think about life and death (who wants to do that?!) and because he understands the drama and passion of bullfights.

Passion?!

I've decided to watch again.

This is the face-off—the final stage of the bullfight. It's down to one bull and one bullfighter—so the pressure is on. I put up two fingers and said, "*El toro y el torero.*"

Grandpa Guy put up three fingers and said, "*El toro y el torero y Dios*" (D Ose), which means, "The bull and the bullfighter and God."

I don't know if God goes to bullfights, but I bet the matador is hoping for any help he can get because he looks pretty puny down there in his tight pants.

He is trying to get as close to the bull as possible without getting gored. He's swinging his cape as if to say, "Here, Bull! Here, Bull Bull Bull!" then standing proud and still as a statue. He's acting as if it's no big deal to be so so so close to a dangerous ton of moving mammal.

Grandpa Guy says he's "confronting death." Me, I'd be running for dear life. I'd be pee-in-my-pants petrified!

The crowd is standing and shouting "*¡Olé!*" (Oh Lay), so we are too.

WOW! The matador just got down on one knee—as if he's going to propose or something! The bull went flying by. Now the matador got down on both knees!! The bull is circling around him! Now the matador is standing up. Wait! What?! He just turned his back on the bull—on purpose! No, don't do that! Turn around!! Phew!!! Now he's puffing out his cape again, as if to beckon the bull to come and get him. Now he's having a private-public stare-down with the angry animal!!

Aaaaaaahh! I can't watch anymore!

Everyone is yelling "*¡Olé! ¡Olé! ¡Olé!*"—especially Matt.

"Should I look?" I asked him.

"YES! LOOK!! NOW!!!" I looked. The matador turned toward the bull and plunged his sword right between its shoulders and right through its heart. The bull fell to his knees instantly and collapsed onto his side! Grandpa Guy called it "a clean and noble death."

The crowd is losing it!!! Ladies are throwing flowers, and everyone is waving white handkerchiefs and white pieces of paper. Grandpa Guy said the crowd thinks the bull's ear should be sliced off and given to this matador.

"Why would he want a bloody ear?" I asked.

He said it's an *honor* (Oh Nor), and he could give it to his girlfriend.

Eww! Eww! Eww! I wouldn't want Miguel to give me a piece of bull ear!

Grandpa Guy said the judge has to make the decision. Then he looked over at the judge and said, "No. No ear."

Now the crowd is mad. They think the matador does too deserve a bloody ear for his girlfriend. Everyone is whistling—even Matt, who is a terrible whistler.

I suddenly feel like a sportswriter.

But I still don't feel like a bullfight fan.

Your friend,

Melanie, who is having an Experiencia

Angel's apartment
unbelievably late

Dear Diary,

After the bullfight, we took a quick *siesta* (Mom made us), and I washed my hair and changed so I'd look as good as possible when we met Miguel and Antonio for dinner.

At the restaurant, at 9:30, Miguel kissed me on both cheeks.

He'd changed too. His shirt was the color of chocolate. It matched his eyes. I was thinking of saying that he has nice brown eyes (*ojos* or Oh Hhho's) but I managed to keep my mouth (*boca* or Boh Ca) shut.

"How did you like your first bullfight?" he asked.

"My first and probably my last," I replied.

"I loved it!" Matt said. "It was interestinger than I thought." He waved his napkin like a cape.

"More interesting," I corrected him. I didn't want Matt to teach Miguel bad English.

"I don't like bullfights,"Antonio said. "The bullfighter is getting paid but the bull is not. The animal suffers for our pleasure."

"Oh, Dad," Miguel said in the same tone I sometimes use with my dad.

"It's animal abuse," Antonio stated.

"We are not vegetarians," Miguel pointed out. "We are carnivores. Why is it worse for a bull to be killed in a spectacle than for a cow to be killed to make hamburger? At least the bull has a chance."

"I like hamburgers and I like squashing bugs," Matt announced, though I wasn't sure what his little contribution had to do with anything.

"Are bulls an endangered species?" I asked.

"No," Miguel said. "The kind of bulls you saw, *toros bravos* (Tour Ohs Bra Vohs), are as different from regular bulls as wolves are from dogs. They are very mean. They would rather die fighting than run away."

Antonio added, "They are bred especifically *for* bullfights." (He said "especifically"—not "specifically." Dad and I looked at each other but we didn't correct him.)

"Bullfighting is not for everybody," Miguel said. "But we don't all have to like the same things."

I looked at Miguel and thought: But yooouuu have to like meeeeee!

Out loud I said, "*Gracias* for the sweater," and gave it back before I spilled anything on it. I'm not exactly known for my neatness.

He said, "*De nada*" (Day Na Da), which means "You're welcome."

Dad added, "And *gracias*, Antonio, for arranging the tickets."

"*De nada*," Antonio said. "If I go to the States, you can get me seats to a . . . boxing match—or an execution. I am kidding, clearly!"

But was he kidding about coming to "the States"? And if he was serious, was that bad news (Antonio visiting) or good news (maybe Miguel visiting)?

Dinner was pork chops. Chop is *chuleta*, pronounced Chew Lay Ta. Matt made a joke about how we could eat them now but chew them later. "Get it?" he said. "Chew Lay Ta?"

Luckily, Antonio changed the subject to movies because it's Oscar time in Spain and America. He and Dad started talking about two Spanish directors—Buñuel (Boo Nyoo L) and Almodóvar (Ahl Moe Doe Var). Then Antonio said I look like a Spanish actress! An *actriz* (Ack Treece)! I'd never heard of her, but Miguel agreed, "May Lah Nee does. It's true."

I smiled and asked, "How did you learn English? In school?"

"School and CNN!"

Grown-ups say watching TV turns your brain into mush, but if you watch in a different language, maybe it makes you extra smart.

Well, it was getting soooo late that in America, people would have been walking out of restaurants, but in Spain, people were still walking in!

Spaniards don't believe in bedtime.

They believe in nighttime.

After dinner, instead of saying "*Hasta mañana*" (Ah Sta Mon Yon Ah) or "See you tomorrow," we decided to take a walk.

People were cooking paella. Outside! Over open fires!

Valencia was having a paella-cooking contest! At 11:00 P.M.!!

I could not imagine Manhattan having a late-night hot dog cook-off.

It smelled *delicioso*, but it was smoky. Some paellas

were bubbling full of vegetables and chicken—yum! Others were full of clams and squid—yuck! Others were probably full of rabbit—sad!

Antonio pointed out a few of the humongous structures that will get burned down tomorrow night.

The streets were so full it felt as if we weren't even walking—just getting pushed along. At 1:30 in the morning (I'm not kidding, that's what time it was), we were in this crush of Spaniards, and we heard a loud *kaboom* above our heads, and we looked up at—

Fireworks! They call them artificial fires—*fuegos artificiales* (Fway Goes R T Fee Syal S). Miguel picked up a flyer and handed it to me. It said (in Spanish) "Night of Fireworks, 1:30 A.M." Can you imagine anything in New York City officially starting at 1:30 A.M.? I'm going to take it to school so I can prove to my Spanish class that Spaniards are party people who don't like to go to bed.

Antonio said these fireworks are *famoso* (Fahm Oh So) and some pilots ask for permission to fly over Valencia so they can see them from above.

Famous? I'd never heard of them, so I thought: How impressive can they be?

I'll tell you: They were amazing amazing amazing!

We stood there, smushed like sardines, looking up at the pink, orange, purple, blue, green, yellow, and red fireworks! Some shot up and came down looking like palm trees or weeping willows or shooting stars or soft old dandelions that you blow on. Some squiggled, some zigzagged; some were fast, some slow. Some went up, came down, then went back up again!

Matt said, "My neck hurts, but I don't want to miss any."

"Same," I said. Then I asked Miguel, "What are the fireworks like on Independence Day?" I hoped that was a good question.

It wasn't. It was a dumb question.

"We don't have Independence Day," Miguel said. "We never really depended on anyone, so we never had to declare independence."

At least he didn't add "Duh." Maybe they don't say "Duh" on CNN?

Dad said that centuries ago, explorers claimed a lot of places for Spain. Years later, those places had to declare independence *from* Spain—like Mexico, parts of the United States, and much of South America. Even Holland used to belong to Spain!

"We are not too good at holding on to things," Antonio said. "But we are very good at living in the moment. We make the most of the here and now." He glanced at Mom.

Fireworks kept going off, and Matt and I kept saying "Oooooh" and "Aaaaah." Mom and Dad did too. But Antonio and Miguel didn't. They are used to incredible fireworks.

"In New York, we have fireworks on July Fourth—when we got independent from England," I said. "Also on New Year's Eve."

Miguel asked, "New Year's Eve?"

"December thirty-first," I explained. "People go to parties, and before midnight, they give out funny hats, and start watching TV and waiting for a big shiny ball in Times Square in Manhattan to go down down down. When it reaches the bottom, everyone shouts, 'Happy New Year!' and fireworks go off."

Miguel said that in Spain, New Year's Eve is called Old Night or *Noche Vieja* (No Chay Byay Ha). People go to parties, and before midnight, they give out bunches of little grapes and start watching TV and waiting for a bell in a clock tower in Madrid to ring in the New Year. When it does, *bong bong bong*, everyone eats one grape for each ring. By midnight, everyone's mouth is stuffed.

"Does anyone choke and drop dead?" Matt asked.

Miguel said people are careful to chew and swallow before they shout, "*¡Feliz Año Nuevo!*" (Fay Leece On Nyo Nway Vo.)

I said, "So you watch a bell and we watch a ball!"

Miguel smiled. "Just so, May Lah Nee."

It is now 3:00 A.M. (!!) and we're finally going to bed. It is so late that Cecily might already be in her pajamas on the *other* side of the ocean!!

When Miguel said, "Good night," and I said, "*Buenas noches*," he kissed me again on both cheeks! (I didn't kiss him back or anything.)

Night-night
Mel-Mel

Monday, March 19

Afternoon

Dear Diary,

If this were a regular day in New York, my school day would be almost over. Since this is spring break in Spain, my vacation day is about to *begin*.

I love vacation!

We slept past noon then begged and begged and pleaded and pleaded and got Mom and Dad to order in from Pizza Hut. The Spanish pronounce it Pizza Hot. It was hot—and good!

In the middle of lunch, we heard an explosion. Matt got so scared, he dropped his pizza on his pants. Smooth move! It was 2:00 P.M., so I calmly informed him, "It's the *Mascletà*."

Dad said, "Mel's right."

"It's the last one until next year because today is the last day of *Las Fallas*," I added.

"Right again," Mom said. "Spring is almost here."

Pizza-Pants Matt made a face at me, and Mom said, "At least you were wearing your jeans, not your good pants." Then she added that "jeans" in Spanish is *vaqueros* (Ba Care Ohs), which literally means cowboys. Cowboys?!

Antonio and Miguel are about to pick us up, so Dad told us to go to the bathroom. Actually, what Dad said was: "Pee now or forever hold your piss—I mean, peace." That got Matt smiling again, but Mom and I thought Dad was not setting a good example.

Secret: I hope Miguel double-kisses me today!

XOXO
Melanie Martin

P.S. Kiss in Spanish is *beso* (Bay So). Is double kiss *beso beso*?

back at Antonio's brother's
@ 3:00 A.M.!!!

Dear Diary,

Two days ago, I wrote, *I could not believe my ears*. Tonight, I could not believe my eyes!

It is ridiculously late, and Matt went straight to sleep, but Mom said I could write until she and Dad are done packing.

First of all, Miguel did double-kiss me!!

(Two exclamation marks for two kisses.)

By the way, in Spanish, exclamation marks go at the end *and* beginning of sentences.

In English, you would read these sentences differently, right?

I like Spain. I like Spain! I like Spain?

Well, Spanish people do you a favor on the *pronunciación* (Pro Noon See Ahs Syown) because they warn you ahead whether to make your voice normal or excited or go up in a question. So it's:

Me gusta España. ¡Me gusta España! ¿Me gusta España?

¿Isn't that cool?

¿Will I be a teacher like Mom?

Anyway, Antonio picked us up and took us to his office. He probably just wanted Mom to see how big his office is. It *is* big, and from his window, you can see the pastry and popcorn stands that go up during *Las Fallas*.

I don't get what Antonio does. I barely understand what Dad does. Miguel asked me, and instead of saying he's an *abogado* (Ah Bo Ga Doe), which means lawyer, I said he's an *avocado* (Ah Bo Ca Doe), which means avocado! I said my dad was an avocado! Miguel laughed but in a nice way.

The bad thing about Antonio's office (and his brother's apartment building) is that when you turn on the hallway lights, they don't stay on long. After a few minutes, they go out to save energy. Mom and Dad think it's a smart system. Matt and I don't because sometimes you're left in the dark in the middle of the hallway. Fortunately, all the switches glow, so when it gets pitch-black, you can usually find one and press the lights back on again.

Still, it can get spooky.

One time I was in the dark right next to Miguel, and I dared myself to reach for his hand—but of course I didn't!!

After we got back to the car, Miguel opened the door for me and said, "After you." Wasn't that sweet?

We drove to a nearby town where *horchata* (Or Chah Ta) was invented. Antonio said, "Me Ron Dah, I remember how much you love *horchata*." It's so weird that Antonio knows stuff about Mom that we don't.

Horchata is a sweet gray drink made from the *chufa* (Chew Fa) nut. It is not an alcoholic beverage so Matt and I got to taste some.

We also ordered a Spanish pastry that was perfect for dunking in our *horchatas*. It's like a donut that is opened and flattened, and it's called *fartón* (Fart Ton). Matt thought that was the greatest word he had ever ever ever heard. He was laughing so hard, I'm surprised the *horchata* didn't come out his nose. He was saying, "Pass the greasy *fartóns*," and "If you eat too many *fartóns*, you'll be fartin' a ton of farts."

Dad said, "That's enough!"

Miguel asked, "What is funny?"

I did not want to translate, and neither did Mom. She shrugged, then said, "Isn't the sunset beautiful?" to get us off the whole *fartón* subject. "Look at those streaks of pink and purple!"

She added that photographers call this "magic hour" because everybody looks beautiful in the fading light.

"I think Me Ron Dah and May Lah Nee look beauty-full every hour of the day, don't you, Marc?" Antonio said. Miguel smiled, and I could feel myself blushing.

Dad said, "I think you Spaniards could give us Americans lessons in gallantry."

I wasn't sure what Dad meant because I wasn't sure

what "gallantry" means (I'm still not). It's confusing. I want Miguel to think I'm pretty, but I don't want Antonio to compliment Mom.

And right in front of Dad!

Then again, maybe it would be worse if he did it when Dad was *not* there!

I checked under the table to make sure Mom and Antonio weren't playing footsie or anything. They weren't. Then I moved my toes two inches closer to Miguel's.

I doubt he even noticed.

We drove back to Valencia and took an evening walk. Mom and Antonio walked in front, then Miguel and me, then Dad and Matt. We all strolled under strings of little festival lights, and it reminded me of Christmas even though Christmas is still nine months (and six days) away. Vendors were selling treats, and Dad bought a slice of coconut rind for Mom, a fried pastry or *buñuelo* (Boon Nyoo L Oh) for Matt, and popcorn for me and Miguel.

Sharing popcorn is my new favorite pastime.

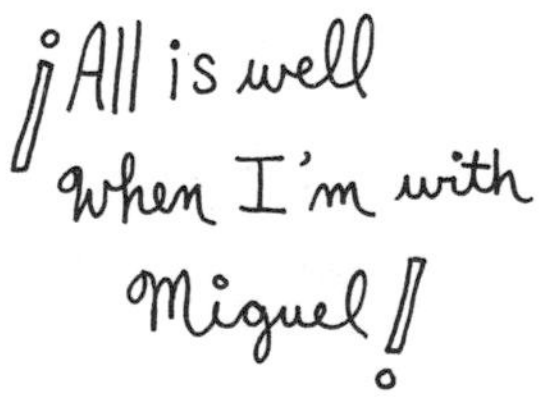

I told everyone to stop so I could take a picture. I took one of everybody, and then in the next one, I accidentally on purpose cut out Antonio—oops! These things happen!

Antonio said, "My turn," and took a picture of me next to Miguel. For about half a second, Miguel put his arm around me! If the photo comes out, I'll show it to Cecily. If it comes out well, I might even frame it!

We looked at more *fallas*—those big wooden things that get planned, built, painted, photographed, and burned to a crisp. I said they were like floats from the Rose Bowl or Macy's Thanksgiving Day Parade—but taller. Dad agreed, but added that some are "political." Antonio said, "Yes. I like very much this one," and pointed out a bullfighter *falla* that was anti-bullfighting. You could tell because the bullfighters looked really dopey. Dad pointed out another one that made fun of the leaders of Spain and of the United States. They all looked dopey too.

Miguel said, "There are also children's *fallas*," and we looked at one with dwarves, dalmatian puppies, and a warty witch holding a poison apple or *manzana* (Mon Sahn Ah).

"Do they get burned too?" I asked.

"Sí, señorita" (See Say Nyor E Ta), Antonio said. "At 10:00 P.M. It's a tradition."

"Tradición," (Tra D C Own), Mom said so we'd learn a new word.

We were eating dinner in a nearby restaurant when Matt asked, "Is it almost 10:00 P.M.?"

Antonio checked his watch and said, *"Casi casi"* (Ca See Ca See) or "Almost almost." (Mom translated.) Spaniards sometimes say "almost almost" instead of just "almost." Isn't that strange strange?

Well, about two minutes later, we heard a big *whoosh* and we could see flames through the window! Someone had lit the children's *falla* right on schedule.

Miguel said, "Let's go look," and held the restaurant door open for me. First the dwarves caught fire! Then the puppies! Then the witch! I'd never seen such a tall bonfire! Lots of people crowded around to watch—couples and old people and kids on parents' shoulders, their eyes all big and round. Miguel and I got close enough to feel the heat. We were surrounded by people, but it also felt as if we were alone—just us.

We were standing as close to each other as two people can without touching.

It was incredible to watch the *fallas* burning, but I kept thinking of how much time and effort went into building them. All for nothing! All that work gone up in smoke!

"Shouldn't there be *firefighters-o?*" I asked.

Miguel laughed and said, "*Bomberos*" (Bome Bear Ose). "*Sí*, there are extra firefighters all over Valencia tonight." Then he repeated, "Firefighters-o," and said, "May Lah Nee Mar Teen, you are very funny."

I smiled. Then I tried to stop smiling but couldn't, so I had to look down at the ground and wait for my face to relax.

Could Melanie Martin be falling in Love?
It's something I honestly hadn't thought of!

The streets stayed full! For the third night in a row!! All the people who had watched the procession on Saturday and the fireworks on Sunday were watching the bonfires tonight. There were also couples and families looking down from their apartment balconies and from behind the iron railings of their windows.

It was fun to be out so late, but I started to worry because tomorrow we leave Valencia. Will I ever see Miguel again? Should I tell him I like him??

No. I'm too chicken, and besides, I read in a magazine that you shouldn't TELL a boy what you feel, you should SHOW him. If you announce, "I like you," you're forcing him to say something. And if he doesn't like you back, you might want to crawl under a rock and stay there for the whole rest of your life.

Even if he *does* like you back, the magazine said, he may not automatically want to say so. Boys don't always want to go public with what's private, and some don't even know how they feel.

So you're supposed to be patient (*not* my specialty). And you're supposed to just pay attention to the boy and try to notice if he pays attention to you back.

The article was called "Don't Rush Your Crush."

The problem with good advice is that it's hard to follow.

I think there are sparks between Miguel and me.

But maybe this whole pyromaniac town is full of sparks because of the firecrackers, fireworks, and fires. Maybe it's nothing personal?

And what about Mom and Antonio? Are sparks flying between Mom and her old flame??

Speaking of sparks, at midnight the adult *fallas* got torched. There were giant bonfires on every corner! And at 1:00 A.M., the ENORMOUS final *falla* next to town hall went up in flames.

I'd never seen anything like it—and for a kid, I get around.

We were squooshed in the crowd again and I smelled the smoke and listened to the crackling fire and watched the red and yellow flames waving in the air like a Spanish flag. My eyes burned as white ashes came floating down from the sky. It felt as if I were inside a snow globe—but a hot snow globe.

Suddenly a cameraman and a lady with a microphone rushed up to me. The lady started talking in Spanish. She was asking, "*¿Te gusta?*" which means "Do you like it?" So I said, "*Sí sí sí!*" She looked surprised and asked if I was Spanish. I said, "No, *americana*

(Ah Merry Con Ah). New York." She said, "*Muchas gracias*" (Moo Choss Grah Sea Ahs), then went on to interview someone else.

"She's getting reactions to this year's *fallas* for TV," Antonio said. "I'll tape the program tomorrow and see if May Lah Nee is *famosa*! I think you will be. If I worked for television, I would like a cute American child to say she liked our *fiesta*."

I wouldn't mind being *famosa*, but I really wish Antonio hadn't called me a child. And "beauty-full" is much better than "cute."

On the walk back, Miguel said, "See how messy Valencia is right now?" I looked at the littered candy wrappers, popcorn bags, and soda cups and said, "*Sí*." The crowds were heading home, and the bonfires were dying down. It was dark out, but besides litter, you could see glowing embers on street corners, like big nests of red rubies. They would have been perfect for roasting marshmallows (especially if you like them golden, not burned).

"You see all those people wearing yellow?" Miguel asked.

Matt said, "*Sí*," and I added, "*Amarillo*" (Ahm R E Yo), because I know how to say yellow.

Miguel said, "Those are our sanitation workers. They work very hard tonight. Tomorrow morning—in just a few hours—this city will be so clean, it will be like all this never happened."

That got me worrying again. We leave Valencia tomorrow morning. Will it be like all this never happened?

Antonio drove us back and dropped us off. Miguel double-kissed me in the dark—I seriously almost melted!

I wanted to ask, "Will I see you again? When? Where?? And do you care???" but I didn't want to be obvious. Besides, shouldn't I be hoping for Dad's sake that Mom will not see Antonionionio again for another 17 years?

Mom just came in and said, "Lights out, kiddo." She and Dad are all packed up. They left Angel some CDs as a thank you along with a note that said to come visit someday.

I better go to sleep before it's tomorrow morning, or as they say in Spanish, *mañana por la mañana* (Mon

Yon Ah Pour Lah Mon Yon Ah). If the rest of our trip is like this, we're going to need a vacation at the end of our vacation!

Love,
Melting
Melanie

P.S. How does this sound:
Melanie Ramón?

March 20, morning

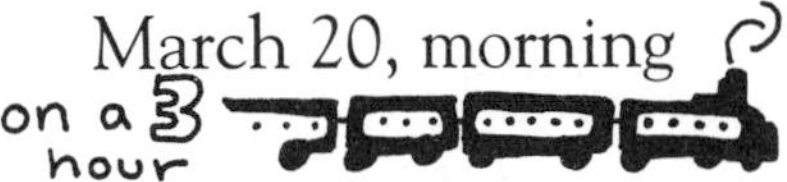

to Barcelona (Bar Say Loan Ah)

Dear Diary,

I should probably feel happy. But it is hard to should your feelings.

The reason I should feel happy (or at least happyish) is that I'm on a family vacation. Outside the window of our speeding train, I can see orange groves and sandy beaches and blue water.

I don't feel happy, though.

I don't feel anything.

Except alone. And very still.

I feel dumb
And I feel numb.
If I were two,
I'd suck my thumb.

We're sitting in our reserved seats. Matt and I are facing Mom and Dad, and we have a table and lamp between us. Dad said, "I can see why you fell for Antonio, Me Ron Dah. He's a real Don Juan. And very gallant. Spaniards put us Americans to shame."

Mom said, "I can't disagree," and smiled.

Matt said, "What do you mean, 'a real Don Juan'?"

Dad said, "A Don Juan is a ladies' man—a player. It comes from an old play by Tirso de Molina (Teer So Day Mo Lean Ah) about a man from Seville who gets women to fall for him but who doesn't know what love is. He's a heartbreaker. Other people wrote about Don Juan too. Mozart wrote an opera called *Don Giovanni*" (Don G O Von E).

"Antonio may be gallant, but he's not a womanizer," Mom said, defending him.

"What's 'gallant'?" I asked. I should have asked yesterday.

"*Caballero*" (Cob Eye Yair Oh), Mom said.

"I don't mean in Spanish! I mean what does it mean?"

"Gallant? Gentlemanly, courtly, having good manners." Mom asked if I'd learned how to say "polite" in Spanish and I shook my head. "*Bien educado*" (Byen Ed Oo Cod Oh). "Well-educated," she said. "Courtesy is big over here. When Americans say someone is well educated, they're talking college. When Spaniards say someone is *bien educado*, they're talking manners."

Dad said, "Didn't you notice how Antonio pulled out the chair for Mom at the restaurant and Miguel lent you his sweater? And Antonio called you both 'beauty-full'?" Dad was making fun of Antonio's accent, which was not *bien educado* of him. "And they were always holding doors open? And they were never just pleased to meet someone—no, no, they were 'enchanted.'" Dad had obviously given this some thought. "Smooth talk and gallantry are second nature to Spaniards. Same with all that air-kissing just to say hello and goodbye."

"Too much kissing!" Matt said. "I could barely breathe!"

"I thought it was just enough," Mom said, and leaned over to kiss Dad.

"How about you, Melanie?" Dad said. "Did you feel smothered?"

He and Mom exchanged a little look. Have they guessed I have a crush?!

I shrugged because I was afraid that if I talked, I might cry. I thought all that kissing was special! That it meant something! Was everybody constantly kissing everybody else and I hadn't noticed?

The train stopped and I looked out the window. People were met at the station by friends and families, and this is what I saw: double kisses and double kisses and more double kisses. It was *Beso Beso* City.

I watched as gallant Spaniards lugged bags for their girlfriends and opened doors for their wives and double-kissed everybody in sight. I even saw one man use his lighter to light a woman's cigarette, which was disgusting but I guess *caballero*-y.

I felt like puking.

Miguel probably doesn't care at all about me.

He was just being polite the whole time! Sharing popcorn and teaching me Spanish and lending me his nice warm sweater. A well-brought-up gentleman, brought up well by Mr. Gentleman himself, Antonionio, the Latin Lover Boy.

How could I have turned it all into a big deal in my stupid head?

Señora Ramón! The 5 M's! It's too humiliating to even think about!

If I didn't have a rule about never ripping up diary entries, I'd tear out all the pages I've been writing.

Right now, on this very train, a girl a few rows ahead just said *hola* to another girl and even they are kiss kiss kissing.

Smack! Smack!
Mwah! Mwah!

Everyone double-kisses around here. It's how they say hi.

It means nothing. *Nada nada nada*.

I feel like an inchworm.

Dad just said, "Who wants to play hearts?"

I shrugged and said, "Whatever."

I may not know anything about real hearts but at least I can play the game.

g2g,

melanie in miniature

Later — almost there

Dear Diary,

Moron Matt stinks at hearts! He can't even remember which card is which! Half the time he mixes up the queen of clubs (a no-big-deal card) with the queen of spades (a terrible awful card).

Playing with such a pathetic player is no fun, so we are taking a break. Dad is now working, and Mom and Loser Boy are playing war. Poor Mom!

Okay, I admit it, I probably wrote the above mean stuff to try to make myself feel better. It didn't work.

Even hearts did not take my mind off my own heart. I could handle it when Dad said, "Who has the two of clubs?" but when Mom asked, "Have hearts been broken?" I wanted to sob.

I'm not sure if my heart has been broken or just bruised, but it's not hearty. It's hurt.

I feel like the jacks look. Which is heavyhearted. The kings and queens look depressed too. I can't believe I never noticed that before.

There are probably tons of things I've never noticed. I'm probably not even observant.

Here is a haiku (five-seven-five syllables):

The waves are breaking,
Breaking, unaware that my
Heart is breaking too.

Here is a mini poem (only six syllables):

What I feel:
Is it real?

I am now out of words. So I will stare out the window and watch the indifferent world rush by.

Insignificantly yours,

Minuscule Mel

after 11:00 p.m.

in our *hotel* (Oh Tell)

Dear Diary,

I am trying not to think about Miguel Miguel Miguel.

We taxied from the train station to our hotel, checked into the room we're sharing with Mom and Dad, then went up Montjuich (Moan Joo Each) for a bird's-eye view of Barcelona. From up high, it's a big bright city by a big bright sea. We saw where the Olympics were held in 1992 and we visited the Joan Miró (Meer Oh) Foundation.

"How come he has a girl's name?" Matt asked.

"He doesn't. Joan means Juan or John," Mom said. "He was born in Barcelona, so he has a Catalan name. Catalan is the language people speak around here—along with Spanish."

"Is he still alive?" I asked.

"Miró made it to ninety," Mom said. "He died in 1983 on Christmas Day."

"Before or after he opened his presents?" Matt asked.

Dad laughed even though death is not one bit funny. Mom sighed and said in Spain, gifts are opened on January 6, Three Kings Day.

I know I'm not supposed to say this, but I don't love Miró. As an artist, I mean. Maybe he was okay as a person.

Mom thinks kids should never look at a painting and say, "*I* could do *that*!" But some Miró paintings are just squiggles, circles, dashes, and handprints, and even Matt the Brat could do them!

I made up a poem and recited it.

Like it or not, here is a fact:
I prefer art that's not abstract.
I think Vermeer and van Gogh
Are much better than Miró.

Dad whispered, "Me too," but Mom said, "Miró also admired the Dutch painters."

Just then an art teacher walked in with a bunch of little kids wearing name tags. The teacher talked about a sculpture, then told the kids to close their eyes and tell her what color it is. A boy shouted out, "Blue." But he didn't say, "*Azul*," which in Spanish is pronounced Ah Sool (regular) or Ah Thool (lispy). He shouted "*Blau*" in Catalan, which is pronounced Blowwwww as though you stubbed your toe and were saying, "Owwwww." You could tell he felt all happy and proud of himself.

Life is so much easier for little kids!

Mom said that when she taught preschool art, she loved field trips.

I didn't know Mom ever taught preschool.

Maybe I don't know anything about anything.

Here's the best I can say about Miró: It's easy to spot his paintings. He had his own style of shapes and splashes, so you can recognize his stuff from across a room. And it's worth going up close because he came up with surprise titles like *Woman and Bird in the Night* when he could have just as easily called the same painting *Kid with Flag* or *Toddler with Kite* or *Alien with Bat*.

It reminded me of when no one could tell what the heck Matt had drawn until he told us his title. He'd scribble a sideways oval and we'd have no idea if it was a potato, guinea pig, torpedo, or killer whale.

Dad said, "Miró had quite an imagination."

Matt said, "You can say that again!"

For the next hour, Matt said, "You can say that again!" to everything any of us said. It was amusing—for two minutes. After a while, I started saying things like, "You are a Butt Brain" and "You are an *idiota*" (E D O Ta means idiot), and Matt still said, "You can say that again!" So I did and he did. Finally I decided to ignore him (which I was happy to do anyway).

Mom pointed out a self-portrait that was ugly or *feo* (Fay Oh). It was so *feo*, you'd think Miró would have been embarrassed to call it a self-portrait. It was a scribbled-on brown rectangle with a big circle for a head and two circles for eyes and three sticking-up lines for hair, like the cowlick Norbert used to have when he first came to our school.

The painting was so bad, I found it inspiring:

Even critics must admit
That Joan Miró's self-portrait
Makes the man look like an it.
Is that perhaps a sign of a wit?

If I drew myself on a day when I felt awful, I wouldn't be a Mona Lisa look-alike either. If I drew myself today, for instance, I'd make a big blob, and instead of calling it *Self-portrait*, I'd title it *Niña Tonta* (Knee Nya Tone Ta), which means *Foolish Girl*.

I was starting to feel sorry for myself again when Mom and Dad said, "Time to go!" and Matt said, "You can say that again"—again.

We got in a taxi. I wanted to go straight back to the hotel, but Mom told the driver, "*Pueblo Español*" (Pway Blow S Pon Yole). She said Spanish Town is a fun place to wander because you feel as if you're seeing all of Spain in one afternoon. She went with Antonio years ago.

I wonder how it makes Dad feel when Mom talks about her old boyfriend.

Here's how it makes me feel when I think about

Miguel: like a clover that thought it had four leaves but found out it has only three.

Well, we arrived at *Pueblo Español* and Mom started pointing out stone gates from Castilla and stairs from Galicia and hanging flowerpots from Andalucia and different things from different regions.

All I saw were couples walking hand in hand.

Dad spotted a popcorn stand and asked, "Want some, cupcake?"

"That's okay."

He looked shocked. "You don't want popcorn?" He put his hand on my forehead as though checking for a fever.

"No, *gracias*."

"I do!" Matt said.

Dad bought some, and Matt kept tilting the bag at me.

But I didn't eat any. No little doves. Not one.

I didn't feel like it.

I didn't eat much dinner either.

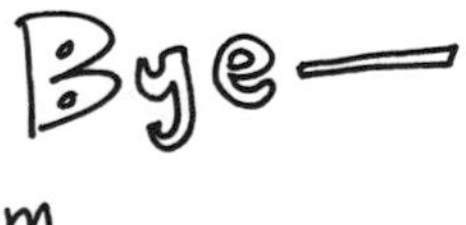

March 21

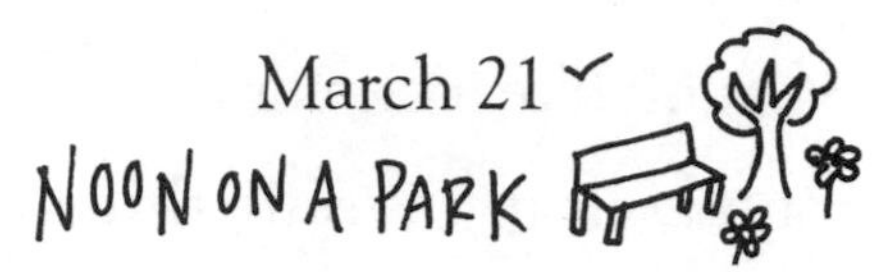

Querido Diario (Care E Doe D R E O),

So far today I'm doing only an okay job of not thinking about Miguel.

It's the first day of spring, but the sky is gray, and it feels as if the clouds are pressing down on me.

I must have accidentally sighed because Dad said, "What's wrong, kiddo?"

I said, "Nothing."

Mom said, "You children aren't getting enough sleep."

That may be true, but it's totally Spain's fault.

Besides, I'm not just tired. I'm deflated. A few days ago, I felt like a big helium balloon ready to soar into the sky. Now I feel small and lumpy. Like a balloon that is resting on the floor and is puckered instead of perky.

Or maybe I'm like an inflated balloon that got let go and went flying across the room making embarrassing farty noises and then landed, dead.

I don't know what Miguel is feeling. Is he thinking about me at all? I keep thinking about him—and trying not to.

I'm kind of mad at myself for caring about a boy I met three days ago, a boy I may never see again.

There are six billion people in the world, and half are boys, and I shouldn't let my mood go up and down because of just one of them.

Not only that, but millions of those billions have problems way bigger than mine, so I should appreciate being alive and stuff.

I can't help it. I still feel sad. *Triste*. Tree Stay. And *invisible*. Een V Z Blay.

I wish I hadn't acted like a big dumb dog with a drooly tongue and a wagging tail that knocks things over. Why couldn't I have acted like a cat—dignified and aloof instead of panting and overeager?

Then again, is it such a crime that I acted happy with Miguel? That I acted like I like him? (I do like him!) If he showed up right now, would I act differently?

It's lonely to feel like this, but I can't talk about it with Mom or Dad or, God forbid, Matt.

They are distracted anyway. We are spending today finding out about a "genius architect" named Gaudí (Gow Dee). Rhymes with howdy.

Gaudí didn't believe in right angles or matching sides. He thought symmetry was boring. Mom pointed to a bunch of buildings and said, "Which one is by Gaudí?" I was about to say, "Who knows and who cares?" but then the answer was suddenly obvious: Every building went straight up and down except one, which was like a gloppy sand castle. Mom said Gaudí treated steel as if it were Play-Doh. She bought post-cards of his work and said she was going to get clay for her students and dedicate a class to Gaudí.

One of Mom's Spanish friends from when she lived here picked us up at our hotel and is taking us around. She is short and nice and she knows all about Gaudí. Her name is Pilar (Pee Lar). Matt calls her Pee-pee Lar—but not to her face!

Pilar took us to the pretty—and pretty strange—place where we are now, Park Güell (Gwell). It looks modern, but it's over a hundred years old! It has fancy gingerbready cottages with white frostingy roofs stuck with gumdroppy things, like in "Hansel and Gretel." The park also has a big fountain with a blue, yellow, green, and orange ceramic iguana that spouts water from its mouth.

Matt and I loved the fountain, and Pilar bought us each a little stuffed iguana as a souvenir. We said, "*¡Gracias!*" and I let Matt name them Iggy One and Iggy Two, even though I might secretly name mine Miguel. During the day, they are going to keep Hedgehog and Flappy Happy company.

Right now I am sitting on the serpentine bench. It's curvy like a serpent and is decorated with colorful broken mosaic pieces that Gaudí found in garbage cans and kilns of mosaic factories. Mom said it was clever of him to recycle broken pieces so creatively.

If shattered pots can become art,
Is there hope for a broken heart?

Dad and Matt just went to buy sandwiches or *bocadillos* (Bow Cah D Ohs). They're called *bocadillos* because you put them in your *boca*. Spaniards also say "sandwich" but they say it like this: Sahn Weesh.

Pilar and Mom are on a bench next to me talking fast Spanish. I think Mom just said "Antonio." In fact, I'm sure she did.

Faithfully,
Melanie

9:30 p.m.
at a restaurant

Dear Diary,

This afternoon, Pilar drove us to this bizarre cathedral called *La Sagrada Familia* (Lah Sog Rod Ah Fah Meal E Ah) or The Holy Family. It might be disrespectful to call a cathedral bizarre, but it *is* bizarre! It has towering spiky spires that look like fat melty birthday-cake candles. (Matt said they look like cacti, but I think he was just showing off that he knows the plural of "cactus.") The cathedral has sculptures that look like they're made of bones and others that look like they're made of drippy wax.

Between the fireworks and *fallas* in Valencia and the Gaudí buildings in Barcelona, all we do in Spain is look up. I'm surprised we don't have cricked necks.

Gaudí was obsessed with the cathedral and worked on it day and night for decades. He practically stopped shaving and changing his clothes. One afternoon, on June 7, 1926, when he was already an old geezer, a horrible thing happened. He was taking a walk, and he got hit by a tram—and dragged along! Since he didn't look that great (because of the accident and because he had been neglecting his personal hygiene), no one recognized him or realized who he was. He wound up in a not-very-good hospital, and by the time people figured it all out, Gaudí the genius was Gaudí the goner.

Barcelona felt so bad that they gave him the biggest funeral ever. Mourners lined up for miles, and the pope gave permission for Gaudí to be buried under the cathedral. (Matt loved the creepy underground crypt where Gaudí is buried.)

When Gaudí died, some architects wanted to finish the cathedral exactly the way Gaudí wanted it, but others wanted to do it their own way. Then the Spanish Civil War started, and everyone ran out of money. Now, over a century later, the building is part old, part new, and still not finished.

"I hate unhappy endings!" I said to Pilar.

"But it is *not* the end," she said. "People are still finishing Gaudí's work."

Inside the cathedral, workers with clipboards and hard hats were cutting stones to build new pillars. The pillars looked like tree trunks with concrete leaves that branched out to hold up the ceiling. Outside, cranes were lifting huge cut stones and putting them into place as though constructing a giant Lego project.

"You see?" Pilar said. "It is not over."

I wonder if Miguel has seen this. I wonder if he considers it bizarre or beauty-full. I wonder if our story is over.

I wish I had a remote control for my brain so I could change the channel.

Gaudí was obsessed by a cathedral! That was noble.

I'm obsessed by a boy. That's *estúpido* (S 2 Pee Dough).

I'd like to get my brain back because right now I think about Miguel every other minute. What did I used to think about all day??

What worries me is this: It might be harder to fall out of love than to fall in. And falling in love is fun, but once you start caring about someone, then you have something to lose, so falling out of love is unfun (even if that's not a word).

Well, we are now at a restaurant Picasso liked that has a Catalan name, *Els Quatre Gats* (Ahls Qua Tra Gots). Pilar ordered us appetizers: toast rubbed with ripe tomatoes and thin thin thin slices of *jamón jamón jamón*. Of course I kept daydreaming (eveningdreaming?) about Miguel and remembering when he said I was a good student!

Are my feelings all one-way?

Pilar also ordered something that looked exactly like fried onion rings. I plopped one in my mouth but it was surprisingly chewy. Finally I asked Mom why Spanish onion rings are so chewy and she said, "Those aren't onion rings, honey. They're *calamari* (Ca La Mar E). Squid."

SQUID?! ICK!
Ugh! Ptooey!!

Is nothing what it seems??

Pilar is now yakking away about another "remarkable architect," Frank Gehry. Rhymes with hairy. He's American, not Spanish. He won a contest to design an art museum in Bilbao (Beel Bow, rhymes with Bow Wow). He made it out of a material called titanium that is super strong but thin as tissue. Pilar thinks it's a shame that we can't go up north to see it. She said that when Gehry doodles, he never lifts his pen from the paper.

Mom said, "Maybe someday we'll come back to Spain and see it."

I wonder if we can come back. I wonder when.

Your obsessed friend,

Melanie Martin

P.S. I signed my name the FrankGehry way without liftingupmypen. I also told Mom she should have her students drawlikethat.

bedtime

Dear Diary,

I wrote a geography poem:

I wish Iberia
Didn't feel like Siberia.

loveless,
Melancholy Mel

March 22 morning
at the hotel

Dear Diary,

Since Matt is taking *forever* to get dressed, Dad started telling us all about Spanish explorers in the New World: "Columbus, Cortés, Pizarro, Balboa, and of course good old Ponce de León, who was looking for the Fountain of Youth."

"Did he find it?" Matt asked.

"He found Florida!" Dad replied.

I like when Matt asks not very smart questions because I don't always know the answers either.

"Was the New World really new?" Matt asked.

Mom smiled. "Not to the people living there!"

"The Native Americans," I said.

"Columbus called them Indians. Know why?" Dad asked.

"Why?" Matt asked, still tying his shoes in slow motion.

"Well, Columbus was trying to find a shortcut to the Far East—to China, Japan, and India, right? But he didn't know that if you leave Spain and go west, you bump smack into America. He made the trip four times without ever realizing that what he'd 'discovered' was a whole new continent!"

"He called the people Indians because he assumed he'd reached India," Mom explained.

"Don't you think that's kind of funny?" Dad asked.

"What?" I said. "I don't get it."

"Neither did Columbus! *He* didn't get it. Today, there are cities and streets named after him, and statues of him on both sides of the Atlantic, and he even has his own personal holiday. But Columbus himself didn't have a clue about where he'd landed. He'd jumped to conclusions!"

I didn't say that I didn't think that was funny—because I had jumped to conclusions too.

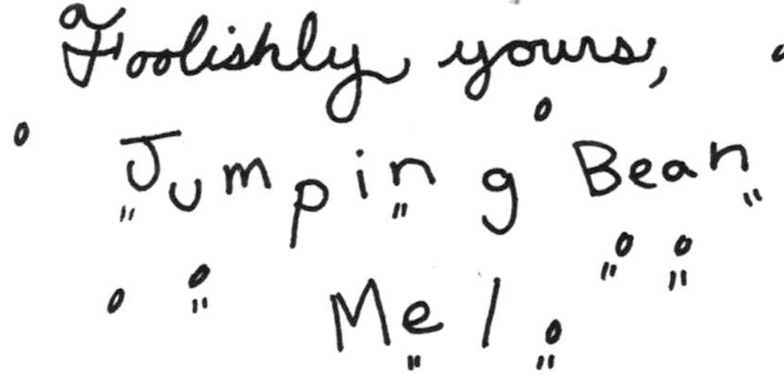

(whose only discovery is that she's clueless)

P.S. I wish I could stay in bed all day but Mom and Dad would never let me.

March 22

breakfast outdoors

Dear Diary,

Chocolate in Spanish is spelled the same way as in English, but it's darker, thicker, and pronounced Cho Co La Tay. Columbus brought it back from the New World. He also brought back parrots, pumpkins, peppers, potatoes, and things that don't start with p.

It's strange to think that I am in the Old World.

Besides hot chocolate, we had bread and potato omelette for breakfast. We are sitting at a table under a big green umbrella on a big wide mile-long street and walkway called *Las Ramblas* (Lahs Rom Blahs). Dad said it's like the Broadway of Barcelona.

He and Mom have spread their city map out like a tablecloth. They're trying to come up with a "game plan," so Mom handed us some postcards and pens to keep us occupied.

Matt decided to write his girlfriend and I helped him with spelling.

He wrote: *Dear Lily, Barcelona is beautiful and so are you. Love, Matt.*

He gave it to Mom and she smiled and said she'd mail it.

I decided to write Miguel.

I wrote: *Dear Miguel, I can't stop thinking of you. Are you thinking of me? It was so so so fun to be with you in Valencia that now Barcelona feels empty even though it is crowded. I miss you. Do you miss me? Love, Melanie.*

Before I handed it to Mom, I reread it. It took about two seconds to realize I could NEVER send anything so gushy to someone who might not even like me back, so I ripped it into little pieces and tried again.

I wrote: *Dear Miguel, I am confused. It seemed like you liked me, but maybe you were just being polite? I hope you like me. Do you? Please write and tell me exactly how you feel.* Gracias. *Cluelessly yours, Melanie.*

I reread that and realized it was as dumb as the first one and I could never send it in a million years. So I ripped it into a million pieces. And started over.

I wrote: *Dear Miguel, Last night we ate ham and it reminded me of you. Your friend, Melanie.*

Well, I didn't even have to reread that to know it was hopeless and I was beyond pathetic. I was turning the postcard into confetti when Dad said, "What are you doing?"

"Those postcards are for sending, not shredding," Mom said.

"They cost money!" Dad said.

"I picked them out carefully," Mom added.

"I hope you have an explanation," Dad threw in.

My throat felt all closed up, and my eyes were stinging, and I didn't want to talk, but I blurted, "I'm trying to write Miguel, and it keeps coming out wrong!" I felt S 2 Pee Da admitting this, but it was also a relief to tell the truth. "I'm sorry I wasted so many postcards."

Whenever I say sorry, Mom and Dad get less mad. Since I knew how to say it in Spanish, I even added, "*Perdón*" (Pair Doan) and "*Lo siento*" (Low Syen Toe).

Mom put her hand on my arm. "It's okay, sweet pea. Why don't you write Cecily instead? That should be easier. Besides, in two days we'll see Antonio and Miguel in Madrid, so you can tell him whatever you wanted to write him."

"We will?" I said, trying to make it sound like it was no big deal.

"You didn't know that?"

"No." Did everyone else? I think Dad didn't because he looked pretty surprised.

"I must have finalized those plans in Spanish," Mom said casually. "Antonio is taking Miguel to Madrid to see his grandmother for her birthday, so we're meeting them in the Prado (Pra Dough). It's an art musuem."

"The Prado!" I tried not to smile tooooooooooo wide.

Then I did write Cecily.

I wrote, *Dear Cecily, Spain is wonderful!!! I have a LOT to tell you. XOXO, Mellie.*

I was going to add *Wish you were here*, but then I thought that maybe it's just as well that she's not this time. I did add *Say hi to your mom* because, since it was a postcard, I figured her mom might accidentally read it.

After that, I was in such a good mood, I offered to play War with Matt while Mom and Dad paid for their *café*. I even taught Matt how to shuffle.

Dad just said, "Who's ready to go exploring?"

"Me," Matt said.

"Me too," Mom said.

"Me three," I said.

We are outta here!

Our first stop will be a big statue of Columbus standing on top of a tall column and pointing out to sea.

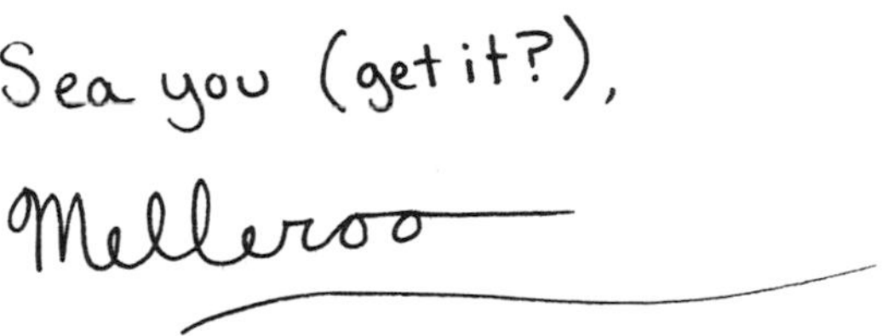

3:22 on 3/22!

at the aquarium cafeteria

Dear Diary,

I feel so much lighter!!! It's as if I'd been carrying around a backpack full of books and I just put it down.

Can I tell you something? (Of course I can, you're my diary!)

Today I am LETTING myself think of Miguel, which is tons more fun than trying NOT to think of Miguel.

Miguel, Miguel, Miguel.

MIGUEL, MIGUEL, MIGUEL!!!

A week and a half ago (seems like years ago), Mom's old roommate Lori said that when she was my age, she was "boy crazy." She asked if I had a boyfriend or "a boy on the brain." I thought those were stupid questions—not to mention none of her business. Now I think they are okay questions—but still none of her business!

I wrote a poem.

Here I am surrounded by fish.
Shall I reveal my secret wish?
I hope that mañana in Madrid,
Miguel can see I'm not just a kid.

Well, all four of us (it seemed like five because of Miguel) got on a moving sidewalk. It felt as if we were underwater, as if we were moving through a glass tunnel inside the ocean! Behind the glass was a whole busy fishy world. Fish were darting around us and above us. Sharks swam by with their sharp teeth and slitty eyes and pointy snouts.

A teeny bit of me worried that if there was a crack in the glass, we'd get sopped and soaked and bitten and eaten. But when I said so, Dad said, "Melanie, for heaven's sake, quit worrying!" It was weird though. It was as if Dad got in a bad mood right when I got in a good mood.

Matt, meanwhile, was in kid heaven. He loved the jellyfish, which I don't think look like jelly. In Spanish, they're called *medusa* (May Doo Sa), but I don't think they look like snake-haired ladies either. I think they look like baby parachutes.

We also saw piranhas, which Matt said eat fish, bugs, frogs, and lizards, but rarely people. Matt's favorite fish, an ocean sunfish, looks like a half fish. It is big, but its body ends in the middle. It looks as if a whale has bitten off its butt.

Maybe when I see Miguel again, I'll ask if he has been here. "Aquarium" is almost the same in Spanish. It's *acquario* (Ah Quah Ree Oh).

I just realized something. If Antonio and Mom had gotten married, Miguel and I would be brother and sister—except not really because neither of us would be here at all.

Did I just write that?

I'm glad my parents can't read my mind. They might lecture me about how there are "lots of fish in the sea." Or they might be mad that they took me halfway around the world and all I can think about is one boy or *chico* (Cheek Oh).

Then again, maybe Mom knows what that's like. Maybe Dad does too—only in his case, one girl.

Mom said, "Let's go," but Matt asked, "Why can't we spend all day here?" Dad answered, "I need some fresh air." He wants us to take a walk on the beach.

Matt said he isn't leaving until he says goodbye to the half fish.

Dad said, "Then make it snappy."

Matt said, "I can't because it's not a snapper."

Dad said, "N-O-W!"

At least boy crazy is halfway normal. Fish crazy is . . . *un poco loco*!

By the way, the word fish is *pez:* Pess in Spanish, Peth in lispy Spanish. But that's only when it's swimming! Once you've fished a fish and it's dead and ready to get eaten, it's not "fish" or *pez* anymore. It's "fished" or *pescado* (Pess Cod Oh).

Some people think Spaniards lisp a lot because they had a king who lisped. Mom said that's a myth.

L8R—

Mellie the Linguist

(that's someone who studies languages)

P.S. I found out that in Spain women keep their names when they get married, and kids use both their parents' names. If Miguel and I had a girl, her name in Spain could be, for instance, Olivia Ramón Martin, which I think sounds very pretty. Matt said that if he and Lily had a boy, his name in America could be Martin Martin. I told Matt that sounds S 2 Pee Dough, but he said he liked it.

same day

on a [bench] in the Picasso Museum

Dear Diary,

On the beach, Matt and I waved to Lily and Cecily. But Dad got out a map and showed us that we were waving to Italy—not New York. Barcelona is on the Mediterranean Sea—not the Atlantic Ocean.

Sea in Spanish is *mar*, pronounced like Mars without the zzz.

"The *mar* is friendly, isn't it?" Matt asked.

"What do you mean?" I said.

"Look, it's waving!" Matt said, and cracked up.

I rolled my eyes and kept walking. The air smelled salty, and the sun was warm on my shoulders, and the sand squished under my toes. It felt more like summer vacation than spring break. I looked at the sea and part of me wanted to get wet, but part of me wanted to stay dry. Sometimes I feel that way about growing up—like part of me can't wait to be older, but part of me wants to be eleven forever.

We came to this big rope sculpture, like a giant friendly spiderweb, and climbed on it. Matt reached the tip-top and bellowed, "Ahoy, mates! Land ho! Land ho!"

Matt the Brat pretended to be
Christopher Columbus out at sea.
He stood and shouted, "LAND HO! LAND HO!"
Till Mom and Dad called, "C'MON! LET'S GO."

We also walked around the narrow winding streets of the old quarter—the *Barrio Gótico* (Bah Rrree Oh Go T Co). We even saw the big stone staircase where Columbus officially told Queen Isabella and King Ferdinand about his discoveries (even if he didn't know what he'd discovered).

He had to report to Queen Isabella because she gave him the money to sail west when no one else would. At first everyone had thought Columbus's idea was dumb. Dumb because what if you couldn't get there from here? And what if there were sea monsters who ate up ships and sailors?

But Queen Isabella took the risk and Columbus took the money. He hired about ninety brave crewmen to go with him out to sea on the *Niña*, the *Pinta*, and the *Santa María*.

It turned out to be good for the queen because Spain wound up with a ton of gold and land. Good for Columbus too because he got promoted from captain to admiral!

Mom said she admired Admiral Columbus for thinking outside the box.

Matt said, "What box?"

Mom said, "He thought for himself. He did things his way."

I tested out the words "admirable admiral, admirable admiral, admirable admiral" and told Matt it was a tongue twister. Then we both started saying it over and over.

We are now in the Picasso Museum or *Museo* (Moo Say Oh).

Picasso spent a lot of time in France but was born in Málaga, Spain. He thought outside of boxes too. His dad taught art—like my mom. Picasso was a natural born *artista* (R T Sta). Even when he was little, his doodles of doves and bulls were amazingly good. By the time he died at age 92, he had painted tons of paintings in tons of styles—and made ceramics and sculptures. Mom said lots of people consider Picasso (Pee Ca So in Spanish) the best painter of the twentieth century. That's the whole entire 1900s!

Picasso is not just so-so.
NO, NO, NO! He's fabuloso.

You know how some of his paintings are of blue people or pink people or big people or pointy people or monkey-face people or people with mismatched eyes or broken-up bodies? Well, this museum is full of his early stuff and it is *not* all abstract. We saw an oil painting of his mom that was completely lifelike.

Picasso once said, "I could paint like a master when I was young. It took me all my life to learn to paint like a child."

When he really was a child, Picasso doodled right in his schoolbooks. I don't know if he got in trouble, but now those books are under glass! I saw one that had a drawing of bulls mating!

Matt keeps acting inappropriate. For example, he whispered, "Look, that's a *boy* horse! You can tell!"

Dad got annoyed (he's been a grouch since breakfast), so Mom gave us paper and colored pencils and told us to pick a painting and sketch it. Matt worked on one of a pretty lady with a minotaur (that's a man with the head of a bull). I worked on one of a pretty lady wearing a *mantilla* or Mon Tee Ya (that's a kind of veil).

Mom said Picasso liked painting women, and Dad

mumbled that he liked women in general—"another Don Juan." I couldn't tell if Dad was sort of criticizing Picasso, or somehow Antonio.

Mom started naming Picasso's girlfriends and wives: Fernande, Eva, Olga, Marie-Thérèse, Dora, Françoise, Jacqueline.

"That's a lot of ladies!" Matt said.

"He was not a one-woman guy," Mom agreed.

Quiet Questions: Is Mom a one-man woman?
Is Miguel a one-girl guy?
Is Dad mad?

While I have been writing in you, Matt has been copying a second painting. It's of Columbus on his column.

"That stinks!" I said. "It looks like he's going to fall. You made him look scared of heights."

Matt stuck out his tongue and said, "Yeah, well, I know who you like."

I did not say *anything*. I just clamped my hand on his *boca*. You know what he did? He licked me! Since I did not want nasty little-boy saliva on my palm, I let go.

"Miguel!" Matt blurted out. "You like Miguel!"

"You're *loco*!" I said. "¡LOCO!"

"I could tell him," Matt the Brat said. But out of the blue, Matt the Brother said the very same words in a nice way. "Really, Mellie, I could tell him. It could help."

"DON'T YOU DARE!!" I said.

Now I don't know whether to worry about Miguel liking me or about Matt telling Miguel that I like him.

Worried Either Way,

MiXed-Up Mel

Same old museum, brand new 

Dear Diary,

We are upstairs looking at a bunch of paintings Picasso did in 1957 based on a masterpiece Velázquez (Vuh Lahs Kez) did 300 years earlier. In Madrid, we will see the real live masterpiece—with Miguel!! Mom arranged for us all to meet in front of it. Tomorrow!!! The masterpiece is called *Las Meninas* (Lahs May Nee Noss) or, in English, Maids of Honor or Ladies in Waiting.

Am *I* a lady in waiting???

I am now gluing in two postcards side by side because it is so cool how Velázquez and Picasso painted the same scene so differently.

Picasso painted it about fifty times, in his own Picasso-y way.

Velázquez painted it only once, toward the end of his life. His main job was to paint King Philip IV and his family. But Philip or *Felipe* (Fay Leap A) was a pale, big-nosed, funny-looking guy with bad hair, so even Velázquez could not make him look majestic.

Mom said that in *Las Meninas*, Velázquez "did something daring." Instead of painting a nice respectful close-up of the king and queen, he painted *himself* painting the king and queen. It's really a painting of Velázquez in his studio with a five-year-old royal girl in a puffed-out skirt, a countess, a dwarf, maids, and a dog. Maybe they were there because they had a question for the king. Or

maybe they just liked hanging around watching Velázquez paint. (There was no TV back then.) "Look carefully," Mom said, pointing to a replica of the Velázquez painting. "See the reflection of the royal couple in the mirror in the back of the painting—?"

Matt interrupted. "But what's so daring?"

"Think of it," Mom said in Art Teacher Mode. "He painted himself giant and handsome, and he painted the king and queen small and blurry."

"They do look pretty puny," Matt said.

"And fuzzy," I added.

"See the dwarf?" Mom said. "Dwarves sometimes lived at palaces and waited on royalty."

"How come?" I asked.

"Because people didn't think royal children should have to look up to anybody," Dad answered. "Especifically not servants." He said "especifically" the Antonio way.

"Exactly!" Mom continued, "I love this painting, and this sneak peek inside Velázquez's studio is much more interesting than yet another formal portrait."

Do diaries give sneak peeks too? Scrapbooks have

mostly happy photos, as though every day is perfect. But diaries capture the commotion of real life.

Matt said, "I'm going to do a Martin painting of the Picasso painting of the Velázquez painting."

Mom laughed. "Go to it." She said other artists had copied *Las Meninas* too.

Meanwhile Mom and Dad and I looked at all the ways Picasso had painted the scene. He analyzed the Velázquez painting from every possible angle, backward and forward, top to bottom.

You know what? I think I've been analyzing my time with Miguel every which way too.

I've thought about how he put his sweater around me and, for half a second, his arm around me. I've thought about every one of those double kisses. I've thought about how our fingers touched in the popcorn. And how close we sat in the car. I've thought about how he called me May Lah Nee and said I was a good student and that I was funny. I've pictured how he offered me food on toothpicks and how he agreed that I look like an actress and how we watched the fireworks and bonfires.

I've gone over and over all those memories, and now I'm worried that I'm wearing them down and using them up! At first, every single time I'd think of one of those double kisses, I'd practically melt. Then, when Mom and Dad explained about gallantry, I practically wept. And now, when I think of everything Miguel and I said, it no longer makes me sigh or cry or want to die (another almost poem). It just makes me want to see him again and make new memories.

And I will — ¡¡Mañana!!

XO,
MM

March 23 morning

DD,

We're up in the air. Mom and Dad are reading, and Matt is sitting in between them, coloring on a barf bag.

Last night in our big hotel room in Barcelona, Matt

and I shared one double bed and Mom and Dad shared another double bed. Matt fell asleep right away, but Mom and Dad whisper-argued for a really long time. They must have thought I was asleep too, but they'd jumped to conclusions.

I couldn't understand everything they were saying (even though it was in English), but I did hear Dad say that it was news to him that we were going to see Antonio again, and that three days and nights should have been *plenty*. Mom said the second visit should not have come as a surprise. "I made it clear to you all along that Antonio would also be in Madrid."

"Clear as mud," Dad whispered.

"What is the big deal anyway?" Mom said.

"This is a business trip and a family vacation—not a getaway for you and your old boyfriend."

"Oh, honestly, Marc!"

"I *am* being honest, sweetheart. Are you?"

"You know I am! And it's thanks to Antonio that we got to see a part of Spain that most tourists never—"

"Well, I'm forever grateful. But Madrid we could have handled on our own."

Mom and Dad went on and on. If their children weren't two feet away, they probably would have been shouting instead of whispering.

My bed was comfortable, but it was uncomfortable lying in the dark listening to them fight. I felt so alone, I almost woke up Matt the Brat.

I didn't even know whose side to be on! *Had* Mom mentioned that we'd see Antonio in Madrid? Maybe. Back in New York, she had talked a lot about the trip, but I didn't pay attention to every detail. Dad probably didn't either. (I hadn't even known that Antonio had a son!)

I feel bad for Mom and Dad, but guilty too because:

The news that upset Dad
Is news that made me glad.

Trust me, feeling bad and guilty and glad (and excited and worried) all at the same time makes it hard to fall asleep.

I must have, though, because at seven this morning, room service woke us all up, knock knock knock, ready or not. But we had *not* ordered room service!! The hotel man realized his mistake and sort of backed out, saying, "Sorrrrry."

If you think that helped Dad start the day better, you are mistaken!

Next thing you know, we were checking out of the hotel and checking in at the airport to fly to Madrid, the capital of Spain.

Matt and I had just started playing hide-and-seek when suddenly it was time to board! We couldn't find Matt anywhere. Dad said I should have known better than to play hide-and-seek before takeoff. (Everything is always my fault.) Fortunately Matt wandered back in the exact nick of time.

If we had missed the plane,
Dad would have gone insane.

I guess Dad is mad mostly because we are seeing Antonio and Miguel this afternoon, and he can't be there because of his meeting with the client in Madrid which, he told Mom, "is the real reason we came here, remember?"

I felt like whispering, "Don't worry, Dad. I'll keep

an eye on them." But what if I am too distracted to be a good spy?

Flying to Madrid is way faster than driving. We're almost almost there!

P.S. I'm still deciding what to say to Miguel. I might ask him if he likes Picasso.

noonish
on a outside

Dear Diary,

Matt is doing his pigeon-chasing thing. We're in Madrid's main square, *La Plaza Mayor* (La Pla Tha My Your in lithpy Thpanish). It has archways around it and a statue of a guy on horseback. Matt giggled and said, "I wonder if it's a boy horse or a girl horse." Mom frowned, so I told Matt to shut his *boca*.

Dad said he should take Matt to Brussels someday. He said it has a gorgeous square and a famous fountain statue of a little boy peeing. "*Manneken Pis*," Dad said. "You'd love it."

"I would!" Matt agreed.

We saw a lady walking two dogs on a leash, and Matt said, "Mom and Dad, if you ever want to surprise us for Christmas, you could get me and Mel a puppy. I swear, we would die!"

"Great," Mom said. "Then we'd have two dead kids and a puppy to clean up after."

Dad laughed, which I took as a good sign.

Matt and I are both planning to own cats *and* dogs when we're grown-up. In the meantime, we'll probably just keep begging. That's how we got Mom and Dad to let us have our two new pet mice, after all.

We are about to have lunch at *Casa Botín* (Ca Sa Boh Teen). It's in the Guinness book of records because it has been serving food since 1725. Back then, America still belonged to England—George Washington hadn't even been born!

I'm excited about the restaurant.

I'm more excited to see Miguel.

I hope I'm not too excited to eat!

Casa Botín

waiting to Pay EURO

Dear Diary,

Here's what Mom ate: baby eels (YUCK!) and sea bull (GROSS!). The baby eels looked like gray spaghetti. The sea bull was a giant crab.

Here's what Dad ate: *cocido madrileño* (Coe See Doe Ma Dree Lane Yo). It's a stew of meat and chick peas.

Matt tried cod croquettes followed by wild boar or *jabalí* (Hhha Ba Lee).

I could not even look at their plates!

I ordered salad and roast chicken or *pollo asado* (Poy Yo Ah Sod Oh).

Dessert was cake called *bizcocho* (Bees Coach Oh) and a jiggly custard called *flan* (Flon). I'm going to try to use more words in Spanish so I can have a *vocabulario* (Bo Cob Oo Lar E O) that is *fantástico* (Fon Tahs T Co).

Linguistically yours,
May Lah Nee Nee Nee

Dear Dear Diary,

I'm tired but wired, and I'm going to make myself tell you everything even though it's reeeeally tempting to just jump ahead to the best part.

After lunch, Dad went to his client meeting, and Mom, Matt, and I went to the Botanical Garden next to the Prado. We looked at the tulips or *tulipanas* (To Lee Pon Ahs), then went inside the museum.

I was excited and nervous. Excited for obvious reasons, but nervous too because what if I've been making a huge deal over nothing? I mean, a gallant guy talked to me about dead bulls, lukewarm omelettes, and efficient yellow garbage men, and I've been daydreaming about him for days.

Last month Cecily had a Valentine's Day party and we played spin the bottle. I sat there while people spun the bottle around, and I kept praying it wouldn't point at me. Well, Cecily's bottle pointed to Christopher, so they kissed—I was a tiny bit jealous. Then Norbert's pointed to Cecily, so they kissed—quick kisses. When it was my turn, my bottle pointed to Cheshire, Cecily's cat. Everyone laughed, and I did too, but the truth is: I was RELIEVED! I gave Chesh a big loud smooch.

He started purring! It was really funny.

Today in the Prado, I was excited-nervous, like during that game. Mom stopped to look at paintings by a guy named El Greco (rhymes with gecko), who did long stretched-out people, and a guy named Murillo (Moo Ree Yo), who painted cute kids and sad Virgin Marys.

I wanted to see *Las Meninas* so I could see Miguel.

We finally finally finally got there. *Las Meninas* is over ten feet tall. It's popular, so lots of people were looking at it. But nobody I knew.

Mom pointed out how dashing Velázquez looked with his palette and paintbrushes. She whispered, "Want to know a secret?"

"What?" Matt asked.

"See that big red cross on his black jacket?"

"*Sí*," I said.

"Getting that cross—getting knighted—was a very big honor, but Velázquez got it *after* he'd already finished this painting. It was added on later, either by Velázquez or someone else—it's a mystery!"

"Cool!" Matt said, but I was disappointed. Not in Mom's Art Teacher secret but in Miguel's not being there. Where was he? *That* was the mystery!

Was Mom disappointed that Antonio was standing her up too?

Suddenly, *uno-dos-tres*, guess who came around the corner? Miguel! He saw me right away and gave me a big smile. I thought I would faint! He said, "*Hola*," and kissed me on each cheek and asked, "*¿Cómo estás?*" I said, "*Bien, gracias*." I felt like adding, "Especifically now that you're here!"

Antonio meanwhile double-kissed Mom and Matt, and Miguel double-kissed Mom and Matt, and Antonio double-kissed me. How could I have not noticed this kissing custom? Love really must be blind!

Speaking of blind, it took me a few minutes before I noticed this girl around my age standing right with us. Miguel put his hand on her back and nudged her toward me and said, "I present to you Luisa." He said a few more words I didn't understand, probably because I was in utter shock. I didn't want to meet Loo E Sa! I wanted Miguel all to myself.

"*Hola*," I mumbled.

"*Hola*," she said. She was pretty and petite (that's French for short) with dark eyes and dark lashes and dark hair.

I should have figured Miguel would have a girlfriend!

My throat felt thick and my eyes felt moist and I had to will myself not to do anything really dumb—like cry or *llorar* (Your R). I kept telling myself to be strong and act normal. After all, I had my pride. (Somewhere!)

Miguel asked about Barcelona and I told him that we saw a bunch of Picasso paintings of the painting in front of us. "*¿Te gusta Pescado?*" I asked.

Miguel said, "Do I like fish?"

"Wait, no no, not *pescado*—Picasso!!" I said, and started blushing. "Now I'm *embarazada*" (M Bah Rah Sah Da).

Miguel laughed. "*Embarazada* means pregnant. You mean embarrassed, true?"

True! But now I was embarrassed embarrassed embarrassed because not only had I been kidding myself about how he felt but I'd just asked him if he liked fish and told him I was pregnant! Even though I wanted to go hide in the museum bathroom the way I did in Amsterdam, I made myself keep talking—in English!

"I like *Las Meninas*," I said, and babbled about the blurry king and queen, the dwarf servant, and the added-on cross. I said it was a painting of a painter—a look at real palace life rather than a formal portrait. I even said two things Mom hadn't said: #1, that it looked like the girl has a secret, and #2, that it seemed as if Velázquez were painting us, as if we were in the scene too. I did not add: "As if we were King Miguel and Queen Melanie—with Luisa the dwarf!"

Miguel said, "You said I was a good teacher, May Lah Nee. But you are a good teacher too. I have learned a lot about Velázquez." (He pronounces his name the Spanish way: Bell Oth Keth.)

So Miguel *did* remember our conversation! Had he been replaying our talks in his mind too?

Luisa was quiet and I couldn't tell what she was thinking. Was she jealous? Bored? Miguel said she takes French in school, not English, and he translated what I'd said for her.

At least that's what I think he was saying. For all I know, he was saying, "Be nice to the tourist kid because her mom is friends with my dad."

Antonio and Mom, meanwhile, were admiring a painting of wise old Aesop. She turned to me and said, "I could spend all day here!"

Well, Mom is the real teacher, and she led us to Philip IV on horseback and asked, "What's wrong with this picture?"

"Wrong?" Matt repeated.

"How many legs should a horse have?" Mom asked.

Matt said, "Four!" at the same time as I said, "*¡Cuatro!*" (Qua Tro).

I was going to shout "Jinx!" but "four" and "*cuatro*" aren't really the same word, and I didn't want to sound immature in front of Miguel.

"How many do you see?" Mom pressed.

We all looked again and couldn't believe it! The horse had four legs—and a fifth ghost leg! What happened was that Velázquez painted the leg one way, then changed his mind, and painted it in a different place.

"Even though he painted over the original paint," Mom explained, "as the years went by, that first leg sort of reappeared. The underlying image had never really disappeared! Now it's just part of the painting. That's called a pentimento."

"Awesome!" Matt said.

Antonio seemed impressed too.

Miguel said, "Your mother is *culta.*"

"Cool Ta?" I repeated. "Cool??"

"Cultured." Miguel explained. "She knows a lot about art."

I said, "She's a *profesora* (Pro Fay Sore Ah) of *arte*" (R Tay). Miguel nodded, which was good because I was afraid I might have said that my mother was a professional artichoke or something. I was going to add that she's a culture vulture, but I didn't want to try to explain that.

Miguel said her name, Miranda, comes from the verb *mirar* (Meer R), which means to look. Well, Mom told us to look at some paintings by Goya (Goy Ya). He lived to be 82, but in his forties, he got a disease that left him deaf and maybe *un poco loco*.

"Do lots of artists go crazy?" Matt asked.

"What do you mean?" Mom said.

"Like Goya and van Gogh," Matt said.

"No, Matt. They had illnesses," Mom said.

"Isn't Goya the name of a company that makes beans?" I asked. As soon as I said that, Matt started singing,

"Beans, beans, they're good for your heart!
The more you eat, the more you fart!
The more you fart, the better you feel!
So eat beans at every meal!"

Mom scowled at me as though Matt's outburst were my fault, not his.

I glanced at Miguel and was glad that he and Luisa were talking in Spanish and paying no attention to us. (I wasn't 100% glad, but I was trying to look at the bright side.)

Matt kept singing, and Mom told Matt to can it.

"Like 'canned beans!'" He laughed, so I told him to zip it.

"It is zipped!" he said, checking his pants zipper.

We decided to ignore Matt, and Mom continued her gallery talk. "Goya painted all sorts of different subjects—picnics, kids, bullfights, dukes, witches, giants, and the horrors of war. Look!" She pointed to a painting of Cronos (Zeus's dad) devouring one of his other sons. The dad's eyes were popping out and scary, and the son was headless and bloody.

Matt stopped laughing. "Whoa! Disgusting! Cronos was a god *and* a cannibal who ate his own kid?"

Mom beamed. "I love teaching Goya. He's never boring."

Then she showed us two famous matching paintings. *Maja Vestida* (Ma Hhha Vess T Da) is a woman lying down dressed. *Maja Desnuda* (Ma Hhha Dess Noo Da) is the same woman lying down naked.

Goya painted a Spanish lady
Wearing silky clothes.
Then he painted her again—
But naked nose to toes!

Matt, of course, lost it, and Mom told him he'd better shape up N-O-W.

Even I was a little embarrassed (not *embarazada)*, particularly with Miguel right there. And Luisa!

Mom never finds art embarrassing. She was on a roll and showed us *The Three Graces* by Rubens (three fat naked ladies) and *Children on a Beach* by Sorolla (three skinny naked boys). It was as if Mom were playing Matt's and my favorite museum game, Point Out the Naked People!

"I wish we had time to visit Sorolla's studio," Mom

said as she led us to some old old old paintings that were extremely *extraño* (X Tra Nyo) or strange! They were by Bosch (rhymes with Gosh).

Antonio said, "I love Bosch."

Maybe Antonio is extremely *extraño*?

The Garden of Earthly Delights is a huge painting on three panels that is bursting with naked people, which would have been bad enough—but they are not just naked! There are nude people riding on ducks, nude people inside mussel shells, mutant animals, a man pooping coins, and— Trust me, this Bosch guy went overboard.

"*¿Te gusta?*" Miguel asked. I didn't want to say *no* if Bosch was his favorite painter. But I didn't want to say *sí* if he thought Bosch was a perv.

"It's interesting," I said. "I like Velázquez more."

"Me too," Miguel said. "*Yo también*." (Yo Tom Byen.)

He smiled really cutely and said he was glad to see me again. But then he started talking to Luisa and I kept wishing I could eavesdrop. Or make her disappear!

It wasn't fair! Obviously, Miguel didn't hate me. Why did he have to love her? And bring her?!

Matt the Brat whispered, "I know something you don't know."

"What?"

"What will you give me if I tell you?"

"If you don't tell me, I'll kick you."

"Then why should I tell you?"

"Matt, you Problem Child, just tell me."

"Guess."

"No."

"Come on, Melanie. It's something important. Im Poor Ton Tee."

"That's not even how you say it. It's Eem Poor Ton Tay."

"Do you want to know or don't you?"

"I do. So tell me or I am going to drop you off at the lost and found, and Mom is so busy with Antonionio, she won't even notice you're missing until we're back in New York."

Matt said, "It's only because I'm nice that I'm going to tell you."

"It's only because I'm nice that I've let you live this long," I said, a little too loudly. Matt can get me so so so mad!

"Okay. Luisa is Miguel's *prima* (Pree Ma). Guess what that means?"

The word rang a faint bell. "Girlfriend?"

"Cousin!" Matt said, all triumphant.

I could pretend that I mumbled a casual, "So?" but why would I lie to you, my own diary? I whispered, "Matt, are you positive?"

He said Antonio told him.

It felt right. It made sense. And I suddenly halfway remembered learning that *primo* means boy cousin and *prima* means girl cousin.

I couldn't help it. I started smiling—inside and outside.

I even whispered *gracias* to Matt the Brat!

I looked over at Miguel and you know what? He was looking over at me! We smiled at the same moment and my insides got all happy.

Unfortunately, Mom said it was time to leave. We had to meet Dad for dinner and they had to meet their grandmother.

Fortunately, we are all getting together tomorrow morning at Retiro (Ruh Teer Oh) Park.

I can't wait!!!

Sweet dreams or Sweet sueños (Sway Nyose)–
Melanie the Dreamer

P.S. Dinner was okay. We got to the restaurant at 8:30, but in Madrid, that is sooooo early that the place was empty. Dad got the idea that he and Mom could sit at one table, for adults, while Matt and I could sit at another table, for kids. Matt thought that was great. I wasn't sure.

I'm not a kid. I'm not a teen.
I guess I'm somewhere in between.

March 24 morning
in our hotel

Dear Diary,

Here in Madrid, Matt's and my hotel room is attached to Mom and Dad's. Dad just came in and saw that I'd put my outfit on my bed, shoes and all.

"Get your shoes off the bed!" he said. "They're dirty. They've been on the street."

Matt added, "Walking on dog pee and cockroach heads and people spit and worm germs."

I put my shoes on my feet and said, "Fine!" really loudly. Dad looked at me as if *I* have an attitude problem.

Even though Dad isn't as art-crazy as Mom, he didn't want to miss the Prado. Since we'd already been there, he said he'd go alone after his conference calls and would meet us afterward for lunch.

Mom said, "Are you sure you don't want to come with us to the park?"

"I can walk around Central Park in New York," Dad said. "I can't see *Las Meninas*."

Mom said, "And you're sure you don't mind if we don't go with you?"

Dad shrugged and said, "Suit yourself, Miranda." I thought that meant that of course he minded.

But Mom said, "Well, the kids need exercise and fresh air, and we can't expect them to go to the same museum twice. So if it's really okay, we'll meet you at 1:30. I hope the calls go well."

He nodded. Poor Dad. I keep forgetting that while we're on pure vacation, he has work problems to fix.

Well, we are now about to meet Antonio and Miguel without Dad—again. I am not sure if that is the world's best idea, but I couldn't bring myself to say I'd go back to the Prado with Dad. Especifically since I'm dying to see Miguel!

I wish there were 2 of me!

Sincerely—

Melanie Melanie

1:00 P.M.

on a garden

Dear Diary,

We are about to go meet Dad, but wait till you hear what happened!

Antonio and Miguel met us at an entrance to the park, and we all double-kissed—a dozen kisses all around. Then we walked by fountains, statues, trees, a rose garden, and a glass mansion called the Crystal Palace. Finally we reached this big lake, and Antonio suggested we rent rowboats.

"Remember when we used to do this?" he asked Mom. She nodded, and I started worrying that Dad should not have left Mom and Antonio alone again to relive their lovey-dovey past.

Why did he anyway? Is he trying to show Mom that he trusts her and it's okay with him if she wants to practice Spanish and catch up on old times? But it's not totally okay with him. He's been acting annoyed—or "miffed," as Mom puts it. Should I worry? (I can almost hear Cecily saying, "Don't worry"—but *her* parents are divorced!)

Anyway, we got to the place where you rent boats, and Antonio rented two. He gave the guy some euros, which are pronounced Ay Ooo Rose in Spanish and You're Rose in English.

Antonio and Mom climbed into the first boat.

Miguel got into the second. Then he looked at me with his *chocolate* eyes. He said, "May Lah Nee, let me help you," and held out his hand.

I took his hand.

I was holding his hand!

He was holding my hand!!

We were holding hands!!!

I stepped into the rowboat and it rocked a little, but then everything was calm again. I sat down even though that meant having to let go of his hand.

Matt was standing by the edge of the water, and I was praying that he would *not* join me and Miguel for three reasons:

1. I wanted it to be just Miguel and me.

2. I didn't want to worry about Matt's telling Miguel that I like him.

3. I felt guilty that nobody was chaperoning Mom and Antonionio.

Their boat and our boat were both still on shore, but then Antonio pushed off with his oar and started rowing away—with Mom.

Matt looked right at me and I was thinking, Oh no! when he smiled and shouted, "Mom! Wait! I want to ride with yoooooou!" He may have made himself sound extra babyish, though it's hard to tell.

Mom couldn't exactly pretend she didn't hear him, so she made Antonio go back for Matt. (Hee, hee.) Once Miguel was sure Matt wasn't going to be left behind, he said, "*¿Nos vamos?*" (Nohs Bom Ohs), which means "Shall we go?" and I said, "*¡Sí!*"

I have to say, it was really fun to be alone with Miguel in the middle of Madrid. The sun was warm on my face and the birds were singing and the trees were pink and fragrant and the sky was blue blue blue.

Rowing together
On a pretty lake—
It felt like a dream
Though I was awake.

For a second, I remembered (embarrassing but true) the rowboat scene in *The Little Mermaid* when the birds and sea creatures start singing, "You gotta kiss the girl," but Eric and Ariel don't kiss.

Of course, Miguel and I didn't either!

Miguel rowed us around the lake and he asked me about school. He asked what we were studying in history (*historia* or E Store E Ah). I told him I did a big project on the plague and how it was carried by fleas on rats, and how a long time ago, millions of people, around one-third of the people in Europe, dropped dead from it, and they died so quickly that an Italian writer said they had lunch on earth with their friends but dinner in heaven with their ancestors. There weren't even enough coffins to go around. As soon as I started talking about the plague, I got nervous and couldn't stop, although I was sorry I had brought it up because obviously a deadly disease is not a romantic subject.

Miguel said he wished he'd shown me a Breughel (Broy Gull) painting in the Prado called *The Triumph of Death*. He said it's of an army of skeletons grabbing people and one skeleton is showing an hourglass to a king as if to say, "Time's up!"

"Sounds creepy," I said, and told him about the monk skeletons we saw in Rome. Then I thought: Melanie, talk about something besides dead people! So I asked, "What is your favorite subject?"

Miguel said he likes history and art, but his favorite subjects are English and Spanish. He asked if I'd ever heard of the poet García Lorca (Gar See Ah Lore Ca). I felt bad that I had to say no.

"How about Cervantes?" (Sair Von Tays.)

I shook my head and felt S 2 Pee Da. Two white ducks paddled by, and I pointed at one and said, "*Pato*" (Pa Toe), as though my saying "duck" in Spanish would prove that I had hidden brains. I probably sounded like a two-year-old!

Miguel kept rowing. "Cervantes wrote *Don Quijote* (Don Key Hhhoe Tay). Some say it is the first novel in the Western World, and some say it is the best."

"I've heard of *Don Quixote*," I said. "I just didn't know who wrote it."

"Cervantes. It's a long, funny book about a man who

was a dreamer. He saw the world his own way."

Miguel reached into his pocket and showed me a Spanish euro. "See? That's Miguel de Cervantes. I'm partly named after him."

"Sometimes I'm a bit of a dreamer," I said, though I didn't tell him what I've been dreaming about.

"You're also a writer."

"Who said?"

"Your mom told my dad. I've started several diaries, but I am too lazy to finish them. I think it's great that you keep a diary."

"You do?" I could feel myself blushing. I tried to stop, but it really isn't something you can control.

"*Sí, señorita.*" He smiled and I smiled and for a little while we didn't say anything. But it seemed like a grown-up conversation and a grown-up silence.

Quietly yours—
May Lah Nee

same day
siesta time back at our hotel

Dear Diary,

Antonio and Miguel had lunch at the grandmother's apartment, and we had lunch with Dad at *La Casa del Abuelo* (La Ca Sa Del Ah Bway Lo), which means the Grandfather's House.

Dad was already there waiting, and he called out cheerfully, "So how's your old boyfriend?"

"Not as cute as my old husband." Mom flashed him a big smile.

"Who are you calling old?" Dad said, teasing.

"Whom," Mom corrected him, and they kissed. Not an air kiss. A lips kiss.

They seemed happy to see each other, which was good since I wasn't sure if they were gearing up for another fight. Maybe a louder one now that they have their own separate hotel room.

Dad said he talked to his client and everything got worked out.

"Oh, Marc, that's great! I'm so glad," Mom said.

"It *is* great," he repeated. I bet Dad felt like he'd done

well on a big hard test that had been hanging over his head. He had probably been as frustrated about work as he was about Antonio, but I guess it's easier to be grumpy with your family than to be grumpy with your bosses and clients (or teachers and classmates). I'm not saying that's ideal or anything—just human.

Mom asked if Dad had gotten to go to the Prado, and he said, "I even got to go to the gift shop." Then he shocked us all by handing Matt and me each a key chain with a mini *Meninas* painting on it and Mom a poster of *Las Meninas* rolled up in a cardboard tube.

Awww! Matt and I said *gracias* and Mom said, "This is perfect for my classroom," and ran her fingers through Dad's hair.

I was happy that Dad's work troubles were fixed and also sort of proud of him. If he'd stayed mad, what good would that have done?

Dad handed Mom a thoughtful gift.
I guess he is no longer miffed.

Next thing you know, Mom and Dad were eating grilled garlic shrimp, which came unpeeled with their heads and tails still on them—ugh! They dug the shrimps out (pretty messy) and dropped the shells right on the sawdust on the floor (very messy). Other people were doing that too—Mom said you can tell how popular a bar is by how messy the floor gets. Matt and I mostly ate bread and drank juice. Mom and Dad drank sweet wine. Dad said the Spanish make excellent wines, particularly red wine—*vino tinto* (B No Teen Toe). He went on and on about it.

I like when Mom and Dad are in a good mood better than when they're in a bad mood, so I did *not* want to interrupt to say that his speech about grapes, vineyards, oak barrels, and cork forests was sort of inappropriate family chitchat. Besides, who cares about the taste of *Rioja* (Rrree Oh Hhha) versus *Priorat* (Pree Or Rot)?

For dessert, we went to a fancy pastry shop, *Casa Mira* (Ca Sa Meer Ah), that even the king orders from. Its window was full of chocolate Easter eggs. Easter and Holy Week are a really big deal in Spain. Mom said we could have whatever we wanted, so Matt and I picked chocolate bunnies. (I like eating rabbits when they're *chocolate*!)

I whispered to Mom, “Have you guys made up?”

“Yes.”

“Totally?”

She smiled. “Arguments are part of relationships, lambie. It wasn’t our first and it won’t be our last.”

Matt asked, “Dad, did you get to see that big painting?”

I was tempted to say, “No, dummy, Dad walked right by it.” But I didn’t want to be mean to Matt since he’d been nice to me.

“Of course I saw it,” Dad said. Even he was probably tempted to add, “Duh.”

“What made you ask, Matt?” Mom said.

“You know how sometimes in a museum,” Matt explained, “a painting is missing? And a note says, ‘Sorry, but we lent it out’?”

Mom smiled. She was probably relieved that Matt isn’t as S 2 Pee Dough as he looks. “I’m sure the Prado never lends out *Las Meninas*. Or, for that matter, *Garden of Earthly Delights*.”

Matt seemed confused so I said, “The one with the guy pooping coins.”

“I liked that one!” Matt said.

“They couldn’t wrap up a giant masterpiece that fast anyway,” I pointed out.

“Couldn’t and wouldn’t,” Mom said. “Some paintings rarely—or never—travel. They are really just too old, fragile, valuable, or popular to lend out.”

“Like Picasso’s *Guernica*” (Gair Nee Ca), Dad said.

“Exactly,” Mom said. “It’s in the *Reina Sofia* (Ray Na So Fee Ah), the museum named after the queen who married King Juan Carlos” (Won Car Lohs). The pastry shop had a photo of the king on the wall, so Mom pointed him out. He looked nice. He wasn’t wearing a crown or anything.

“Juan sounds like wonton, like wonton soup,” Matt said.

“Wonton backward is not now,” I added, even though that was off the subject.

“Anyway,” Mom continued, “we’re going to pop into that museum and—”

“Another *museo*?!” I said.

“You can’t make us!” Matt said.

Dad came up behind Mom and put his arms around her. “Kids, I’m pretty museumed out myself, but Mom and I—”

“You have no idea how many wonderful museums

we're skipping!" Mom said, sounding genuinely pained. "I'm afraid this is non-negotiable. We'll see just that one painting, and then," she sighed, "no more art museums for the rest of the trip."

"Just that one painting," I said.

"Swear?" Matt asked.

"Pinky swear," Mom said, and twisted pinkies with him.

"The reason I mentioned *Guernica*," Dad said, "is because it was in New York, on loan at the Museum of Modern Art for decades! Picasso said Spain couldn't have it until after Franco was dead. And Franco took forever to die."

"Who's Franco?" I asked. One of the hard things about getting older is there are so many people you're supposed to automatically know about.

"Franco? Well, there was a civil war—" Dad began.

"A silver war?" Matt asked. Mom and Dad both smiled. Usually I don't like when they beam together over Little Angel Boy, but now I'm just glad they're getting along.

"A *civil* war," Mom said. "Spaniards were fighting other Spaniards. It was very uncivil, as war always is."

Dad continued, "At the end, Franco took over and ruled

Spain for around forty years. He was a dictator, and people were not allowed to vote or even complain about him. You know how in the United States, if you're mad at the president, you can say, 'What an idiot'?"

"*Idiota,*" I said.

"Under Franco, if you said something bad about the government, you could get thrown in jail—or killed."

"Killed?" I asked.

"Killed," Dad repeated.

Matt gobbled up the last of his bunny and asked, "What else are we doing today?"

Dad seemed happy to change the subject. "Well, I tried to get tickets for a Spanish operetta, a *zarzuela* (Sar Sway La), but it's not the season. My client invited us to drop by his apartment before dinner, at eight."

"Great," Mom said. "And Antonio invited us for a light supper at his mother's at nine—"

"He did??" I interrupted.

"But," Mom continued, "it's completely up to you, Marc. I said I'd call."

Dad looked at me and could probably tell that despite everything I was hoping he'd say *sí sí sí*.

"Let's do both," Dad said, and handed Mom a cell phone.

"Wait a sec," Matt said. "How many old people am I going to have to be nice to?"

Dad said we were lucky to be invited places—it meant we weren't just doing tourist things. Mom smiled then called the client and Antonionio. At the end, instead of saying bye to them and hanging up, she said, "***Adiós*** *adiós adiós*," as though the calls were fading away instead of ending. She said they do that on the phone in Spain. It makes saying goodbye seem less abrupt, less final.

At the museum, Mom said we would like the paintings by Salvador Dalí (Sal Va Door Doll E). He had a curled-up mustache, and he painted melting clocks and eggs with flowers inside, and he tried to paint dreams. I was tempted to take a peek, but Matt said, "Mom, you pinky swore." So she marched us straight to *Guernica*, which is a huge mural painted on a canvas.

It is sad sad sad.

Guernica was a regular little Basque town, and one April afternoon in 1937, Franco told Nazi planes to surprise-bomb it. They did—for three hours! The whole village burned—for three days! Sixteen hundred people got hurt or killed. Picasso's masterpiece is black and white and amazing, and it shows a mom holding her dead kid and a person crying out at the sky and a horse in agony. Mom said it helped people wake up to the terrible things going on. Today in New York, a tapestry of *Guernica* hangs in the United Nations, maybe to remind countries to get along.

Matt sat down on the floor—but a security guard made him get up.

"These kids are tired," Dad said.

"We'd better go," Mom said.

"I wouldn't mind taking a nap myself." Dad smiled.

We are now back at our hotel. It is *siesta* time and Mom and Dad said not to disturb them for an hour. Right when they were shutting the door that attaches our rooms, Matt said, "Mel, let's raid the minibar." But Dad overheard him and poked his head in. "If you do, it will come out of your allowances. Those snacks add up."

Well, Matt is now sitting on his bed with Flappy Happy and Iggy One. He is digging out the dirt between his toes. It's gross except that I used to do it too.

I tucked Hedgie and Iggy Two in for a nap. Their little heads are on my pillow, peeking out of the sheets and blanket.

Me, I am about to take a nice long bubble bath. The hotel gave us free soap, shampoo, lotion, and bath oils. All I need is a rubber ducky—*pato*.

in a taxi

almost almost 9:00 P.M.

Dear Diary,

We're on our way to see Miguel!

Mom keeps pointing out how dramatic the lit-up fountains and archways and fancy buildings look at night.

I'm wearing the nicest clothes I brought: a pink shirt, black skirt, and sandals (with no heels because Mom won't let me buy heels, which is unfair, especially since I don't even have pierced ears yet).

Dad's client's name is *Señor* García (Gar See Ah). He speaks English or *inglés* (Ing Lace) with an accent.

He called Matt Mateo (Ma Tay Oh) and said he looked just like Mom. Mom cooed, "I'll take that as a compliment," but Matt grumbled, "I won't." (Dad elbowed him.)

Señor García's apartment has dark furniture and drapey curtains and oriental rugs. He knows Dad likes opera, so he put on a tape of Plácido Domingo (Pla See Dough Doe Mingo) la-la-la-ing away.

There was also a Siamese cat named Bonita (Boh Neat Ah). *Bonita* means pretty, and the cat was pretty. I crouched down to pet her and she was purring purring purring—until Matt started chasing her and she ran away.

I said, "Act your age, not your shoe size."

Matt said, "I *am* acting my age."

The cat ducked—wait, can cats duck? Ducks can't cat! Okay, the cat *snuck* under a tall shelf of breakable figurines but left the tip of her furry white tail sticking out, as if to say, "Psssst, I'm just pretending I don't want to play."

Matt bent down, but Dad shouted, "Watch out for the *Lladró*!" (Ya Dro.)

Matt stopped in his tracks and said, "Huh??" so *Señor* García showed us his really fragile, really expensive collection of porcelain, including a sculpture of Don Quixote that is over a foot tall and has a breakable mustache pointing out on both sides.

Then *Señor* García said, "Seet down, seet down," and poured us some Coke. Mom would never usually let us have Coke after five, but she couldn't say anything since this man's legal troubles are why we got to come to Spain.

He poured Mom and Dad sherry or *jerez* (Hair Ez) and put out bowls of olives and almonds, which Mom and Dad chowed down while we kids went hungry. He must have noticed we weren't eating because he put out a bowl of potato chips, which we scarfed in two seconds flat. I was hoping for a refill but no such luck or *suerte* (Swear Tay).

There was a bowl of red, yellow, and purple candies on top of a lace doily. Matt and I liked only the red and yellow ones—so pretty soon it was a bowl of just purple candies. (Hee, hee.)

Señor García said, "I have been to Ah Mare Eek Ca. Is this your first trip abroad, children?"

I said, "We've been to Italy and Holland."

Ma Tay Oh said, "I have a joke."

Dad looked worried. Mom too. I think they were afraid Matt was going to tell a pee, poop, or fart joke, and since *Señor* García speaks English, they couldn't just say, "No pee, poop, or fart jokes!"

After a pause, Dad said, "Keep it clean, Matt!"

Matt said, "Where do hamsters go on vacation?"

"Where?" *Señor* García asked.

"Hamsterdam!" Matt said. Mom beamed, Dad sighed, *Señor* García laughed, and I just rolled my eyes.

"How old are you, Ma Tay Oh? *¿Cuántos años tienes?*" (Quon Tose On Nyose Tyen S.)

Matt answered, "*Siete anos*" (Syeh Tay On Nose). But Matt hasn't started Spanish in school, and he accidentally said a terrible thing. *Año* (On Nyo) with the squiggle over the n is year. *Ano* (On No) without the squiggle is, I hate to write this but . . . anus! Matt said he has seven——! Well, Mom quickly gave him an emergency Spanish lesson and made him say it the right way.

To tell you the truth, *Señor* García laughed way harder at Matt's mistake than he had at Matt's joke! So Matt, instead of being mortified like a normal person, got proud of himself for being a comedian without even trying.

After a while, we all shook hands (no kisses), went down the elevator, and got in a taxi.

Inside, Mom tilted her head back and said, "I can't believe I'm going to see Antonio's mother again after all these years."

I'd almost forgotten that she didn't know just Antonio—she knew his whole family.

Gotta stop because the taxi stopped!

Yours,

Mel Mel Mel who is about to see Miguel Miguel Miguel

at the hotel

Dear Diary,

Antonio's mom has an awful name. It's Dolores (Doe Lore Ays), which sounds okay in English but means pains and sorrows in Spanish.

Except for her name, I liked her. She is short with fluffy white hair and soft skin. She asked us how old we were and I answered right and Matt managed to say *siete años*. (Phew!)

But then he behaved as though he were only five or *cinco* (Sink Oh).

For instance, when Dolores told us that Antonio and Miguel were on their way, Matt whispered to me, "Remember in the *Snow White* video when Snow White sings, 'I'm waiting for the one I love'? Remember how you used to think it was 'I'm waiting for my one-eyed love'? Wouldn't it be funny if Miguel walked in with an eye patch?" And he kept giggling.

If looks could kill, Matt would have expired then and there.

Dolores led us to the dining room, where the table

was covered with plates of asparagus, white beans, roasted peppers wrapped around tuna, *manchego* (Mon Chay Go) cheese, quince paste, and Spanish sausage called *chorizo* (Chore E So). I was afraid I would starve to death until I saw the potato omelette and bread.

Antonio and Miguel walked in, and Dolores asked Antonio to go to the kitchen and slice off some ham from a big dried leg of pig. Dad said that pigs that eat acorns all day become extra tasty, and legs like that cost hundreds of dollars and last for months. We watched as Antonio carved a piece of the leg into almost see-through slices.

I like ham, especially *jamón ibérico* (Hhham Own E Bear E Co), but it's hard to get used to looking at a pig leg with its black hoof still attached. In New York, you'd never see a shopper hurry home with a pig foot sticking out of a grocery bag.

In kitchens and on plates
In the United States,
We rarely see the feet
Of the animals we eat.

The grown-ups were talking and Miguel turned to me and asked, "You have been here long?"

"Just a few minutes," I said.

Matt added, "She was counting every one, trust me."

I wanted to punch his little guts out, but Miguel gallantly acted like he hadn't heard Matt.

Miguel said, "Your shirt is pretty—*bonita*."

I was considering saying, "Yours too," when Matt said, "We met a cat named Bonita!" and started talking about cats and dogs. Matt told Miguel that he and I want a dog, but since we live in a city, it would have to be walked all the time instead of just let out the back door. "And the person walking it would have to carry a baggie for the poop because it's against the law to leave it in the street, and Mom says that she doesn't want to have to deal with mushy warm dog poop. We said we'd do it, but—"

"Mushy?" Miguel asked.

"Soft and gooshy," Matt explained.

Dog poop?! This was even worse than talking about disease and death!

"We have two new mice and a fish called Wanda," I

said. Suddenly I panicked and asked Matt, "Who's taking care of them?"

"Lily, remember?"

"I hope she doesn't overfeed Wanda."

"She won't," he said.

At dinner Dolores tried to overfeed *us*! Mom said, "This is a feast! So many good things!" She thanked Dolores for going to such trouble and explained to us that after heavy two-course lunches, Spaniards usually have light and simple dinners. (It's the opposite of in America, where lunch is usually lighter.) Dolores said it was *nada*, nothing, and kept encouraging us to eat eat eat. I stirred everything around on my plate, and hid some gross stuff under a lettuce leaf and other gross stuff under a piece of bread. I hoped no one noticed.

Dolores called Mom and me both *hija* (E Hhha). It means daughter, but Mom said it's just a nice thing to say, like honey or sweetie.

The asparagus, by the way, was not skinny and green. It was fat and white. Mom said it's a delicacy. Matt said, "Ever notice that asparagus makes your pee smell funny?" No one translated, and I pretended I didn't speak English. And, no, I'd never noticed because I've never eaten asparagus!

Dad said, "Matt, there will be consequences if you keep behaving like a nincompoop." Bad word choice. I could tell Matt was dying to make nincompoop poop poop jokes but didn't dare.

Instead, he told his hamster joke, which Mom did translate. It is just as funny (or lame, depending on your opinion) in Spanish as in English because hamster is pronounced Ahm Stair and Amsterdam is Ahm Stair Dom.

After a while, I asked, "May I be excused?"

"*Sí*," Dad said.

Miguel asked to be excused too!

So did Matt the Brat.

"May Lah Nee," Miguel said, "have you met Blanquito?"

"Blon Key Toe?"

"Come. I show you."

I followed him into Dolores's den, and Shadow Boy trotted right along after us. Miguel said, "This is Blanquito," and showed us a white bird or *pájaro* (Pa Hhha Row).

Miguel shut the door and opened its cage. Blanquito flew out, flapped around, and landed on my head!

At first I was scared, but Miguel's eyes told me not to be. "*Tranquila* (Tron Key La). It's okay."

The bird's tiny talons scratched my scalp. They tickled more than hurt, but I was still a little worried. Miguel said, "Don't worry. *No te preocupes*" (No Tay Pray Oh Coop Ace). Even though I don't usually like when people tell me not to worry, I didn't mind when Miguel said it.

"Okay," I said.

"She *should* worry," Matt said. "A bird once pooped on me."

I wished I could give Matt a time-out! I can't wait for him to grow out of the stupid stage he's stuck in!

Miguel put his finger by my ear and Blanquito

hopped on. "He's a good bird," he said. "Aren't you, Blanquito?"

Blanquito squeaked.

Matt looked at us and said, "Should I leave? I mean, if you want to be alone? Alone but together? Just you two? I could go watch TV. I like cartoons and bullfights in Spanish. The only thing I don't like is that in some American shows, Spanish comes out of American mouths, but the mouths don't always match up with the words."

If Matt was trying to be nice, why couldn't he have just said, "Where's the *televisión*?" Why did he have to be so obvious—and practically ruin everything?

Miguel said, "Stay with us, Matt. It is no problem." But would Miguel have liked to be alone with me? I was still feeling sparks even though we weren't in Pyrotown Valencia anymore.

"Give me your hand, May Lah Nee," Miguel said, and I handed him my hand. (Can you hand someone your hand?) His hand felt warm and I thought of our Rowboat Moment. He said, "Open your fingers," and I did, and he gently tucked in three of my fingers so only my pointer finger was sticking out. "Ready?"

"Ready," I said, a little nervously. Blanquito hopped *uno-dos-tres* from Miguel's hand onto mine, as though my finger were a twig. He ruffled his wings.

Miguel smiled and I smiled back. It was almost almost as if Matt weren't there. But then Matt took a turn with Blanquito and started yammering about how people say that someone who doesn't eat a lot eats like a bird when in fact, many birds eat half their own weight every day.

When did he become Mr. Know-it-all Science Boy anyway?

Miguel put his finger near Matt's, and Blanquito hopped back on. Then Miguel lifted his hand, bird and all, to his face and made kissy noises. Blanquito started pecking him gently right above his chin—little bird kisses!

Just then Mom popped her head in and said, "Time to go." Get this: She also asked Miguel if he'd like to go with us to Segovia (Say Go V Ah) tomorrow since Antonio would be busy helping his mother with medical forms. Miguel said, "Sure," so we're picking him up at nine. Yay!!!

Right before we left, Matt said, "What about the present?"

"I almost forgot!" Mom said.

Matt and I handed Dolores a coffee-table book of photographs of New York. She said something in Spanish that probably meant "You shouldn't have, but I'm glad you did!" Mom said she hoped Dolores and her family would visit us someday—they were always welcome.

When we all said goodbye, Dolores had tears in her eyes. Mom's eyes were shiny too.

In the taxi to our hotel I asked Mom why she seemed sad. She said, "Dolores was like a mother to me when I lived in Spain. It's hard to see her looking older, and it's hard not knowing when or if I'll see her again."

"She seemed sad to say *adiós* too," I said.

Mom nodded. "There are many different kinds of love."

Love,

Midnight Mel

2:30 A.M.

Dear Diary,

I'm writing this with the flashlight pen Cecily gave me last Christmas. I don't want to turn on the light because Matt is asleep.

I should be too.

But I woke up thinking about the many-different-kinds-of-love thing. And I was thinking that maybe it's just as well that Matt stayed with Miguel and me.

What if Miguel had closed the door and I'd been inside with just him (and Blanquito)?

Would he have tried to kiss me? I don't know if he's ever kissed anyone, but I haven't—unless you count family members. Or Cecily's cat!

I don't know if I even know how to kiss.

For instance, do you tilt your head a little so your noses don't bump? And if so, do you tilt left or tilt right? Maybe you tilt right if you're right-handed??

And do couples who wear glasses take them off when they kiss? (I wear mine mostly for reading and writing.)

Cecily and I once talked about kissing and she said I shouldn't worry because she was sure there's not just one right way. She also said that people don't worry about how to hold someone's hand and where to put their fingers, so she figures some things must come naturally.

Maybe. But what if I mess up?

An Eskimo kiss seems pretty basic: You rub noses.

A French kiss seems complicated and has something to do with tongues. Eww! (Mom once said that Paris is full of couples kissing.)

Now I'm wondering: Is there such a thing as a Spanish kiss?

Do I want to find out??

I don't know!!!

I've also been thinking about the phrase "falling in love." Falling is always a little scary, isn't it? I mean, when you fall, you can get hurt or bruised. So is it possible, instead of falling in love, to step in? Or would it then not be love?

Maybe for some people, falling in love is a perfect swan dive.

Maybe for others, it's a painful belly flop.

I used to imagine I "loved" Christopher, but now I

realize that half the girls in my grade say they love him. And Christopher and I have barely even had a private conversation, just us, that wasn't about homework!

At least now I know what love isn't, even if I'm not sure what love is.

It's confusing, but I feel *un poco* better writing all this down.

Your not-all-that-tired friend—

Middle-of-the-Night Mel

P.S.

When a couple shares a kiss,
Do they each feel utter bliss?
Or stumble in a deep abyss?
Is it sort of hit-or-miss?

March 25

almost 9:00 a.m. at the hotel

Dear Diary,

A fly got into Matt's and my room and started buzzing near my head. I said, "I remember being scared of flies when I was a kid."

"Hate to break it to you," he said, "but you're still a kid."

"I mean a little kid—like you."

He ignored me. He was busy driving his favorite red car around the bedspread.

"Did you bring that from home?" I asked.

He nodded.

"That's pathetic," I informed him, but he kept driving the car around.

He looked up. "Mel, do you think DogDog misses me?"

I was going to say, "Are you kidding? He probably loves having the whole bed to himself." Instead, I said, "Maybe a little, but I bet he's just sleeping extra. When you get back, I'm sure he'll wag his tail like crazy."

Matt's eyes got bright. "Think so?"

"I'm positive."

"Should I send him a postcard?"

"No, Matt. That would be pushing it."

"If you'd left Hedgehog behind," he offered, "she'd just hibernate."

"Hedgehogs hibernate?"

"You didn't know that?"

"I wasn't sure."

"They hibernate in winter. And they have thousands of sharp spines on their backs—but none on their bellies."

"My hedgehog's spines are all soft. Which is good since otherwise I couldn't cuddle her. And Hedgie doesn't hibernate. She sleeps when I sleep and is awake when I'm awake."

Matt shrugged.

"You know who might be missing you a little?" I said.

"Who?"

"Lily."

Matt smiled a dopey smile and parked his car under his pillow. Then he started flapping his blanket like crazy and said, "Look inside."

I looked inside his covers, and every time he flapped the blanket, he created tiny sparks. It was like his own private fireworks. Or like a baby firefly party.

He said, "That's static electricity."

"Cool," I had to admit. And now I'm going under my covers to see if I can give myself a light show.

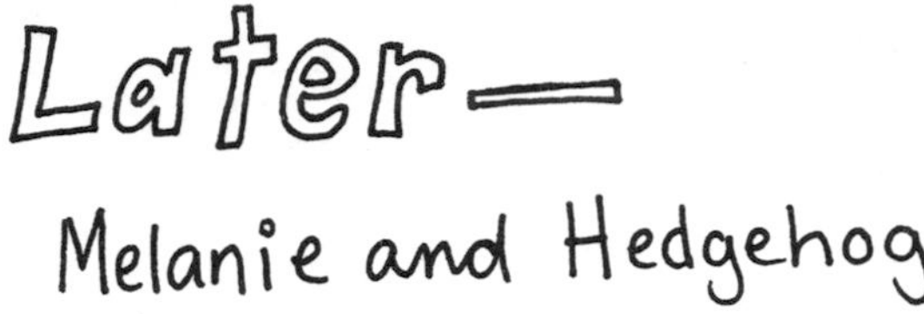

Dear Diary,

Today was jam-packed. It was also happy and sad.

I will start with the happy part.

We rented a car and picked up Miguel, and he sat next to me as we drove north to Segovia.

When Miguel got in, Matt said, "*Bueno dios.*"

Miguel laughed. "That means 'Good God.'" Then he said, "I will help you pronunciate *Buenos días*"—which he did after we helped him "pronunciate" pronounce!

Miguel's and my favorite site in Segovia is its Roman

aqueduct. It has tall double arches that are more than 2,000 years old and almost half a mile long! The Romans carefully stacked all the stones right on top of each other without even using cement. Now cars whiz past the aqueduct like it's no big deal. Drivers barely look up.

In New York, people rush by the Empire State Building without stopping to think, Wow! Architects built this! I guess even extraordinary things can seem ordinary if you forget to appreciate them.

Anyway, we went in Segovia's cathedral and Dad pointed out tapestries, stained-glass windows, and gravestones on the floor.

"Ever heard the expression 'stinking rich'?" Dad asked. "Long ago, poor people got buried in graveyards, but rich people sometimes paid to get buried *inside* churches and cathedrals. Unfortunately, on really hot days, their newly buried, freshly rotting bodies started to smell—to stink."

"Disgusting!" Matt said, gleefully.

"I thought you'd like that," Dad said.

"I have learned something new." Miguel laughed.

Mom led us along a windy path to a medieval castle perched high up on the side of a cliff. Matt asked, "Does medieval mean evil?"

Dad said, "It means from the Middle Ages." He added that Isabella became a queen in that castle in 1474 and that she did both good and evil things.

"What did she do that was evil?" Matt asked.

"They say she didn't bathe," Dad began. "But the really evil thing is that if you weren't Catholic, she kicked you out of Spain—or had you killed. Zero tolerance. Hundreds of thousands of Jews had to leave Spain in 1492. Muslims too."

"The Spanish Inquisition," Mom added.

"What did she do that was good?" Matt asked.

"That same year, she sponsored Columbus, remember?" Dad said.

"1492 was a big year in history," I said.

"I wish I could live in the Middle Ages," Matt said. "I love castles!"

"You're way too late," I said. "And besides, they tortured people and they did *not* have toilets that flushed."

Matt shrugged. "Doesn't the castle look like it's from a Disney movie?"

"Where do you think Walt got his inspiration?" Mom said, pointing out its cool turrets and towers.

Inside, a guide told a sad story about a king and queen who were visiting. Their little son was running around like a wild child and he fell out a window! And died! His baby-sitter was so upset—and worried about what the king and queen would do to her—that she jumped out the same window right after the little prince. She died too!

Matt looked out the window as though trying to picture that terrible day.

Miguel said, "Let's climb to the top of the castle," so we walked up the dark and narrow winding steps. Matt was supposed to count them, but he lost track after 140. The stone steps themselves have gotten worn down from hundreds of years of climbing. Some actually sag in the middle.

When we got to the tippy-top—and daylight—we

looked out at the golden cathedral, green countryside, snow-capped mountains, and big fluffy clouds. Miguel asked Mom if he could use her camera to take a picture of all of us. She said that would be nice, so he took three. It was really windy and my hair was blowing all over the place.

After a while, Matt said he was ready to go, and Mom and Dad led the way back down the sagging steps.

I was about to follow when Miguel whispered, "*Espera* (S Pear Ah). Wait."

I hesitated for a second, then stood still with him on the top of the castle. The wind picked up. He said, "I take another picture." I leaned against the sand-colored wall and smiled (which was easy) and he snapped a photo of me and my windblown hair. Then he leaned against the wall right next to me—we were shoulder to shoulder—and he stretched out his right arm in front of him and snapped a close-up of the two of us together. My whole face was smiling—not just my *boca*. Half of me wanted to say, "We better not take too many photos," but the other half wanted to stay up there forever and blast through rolls and rolls of film as though this were a photo shoot and we were Penélope Cruz and Antonio Banderas, only young.

"Will you send me copies when they get revealed?" Miguel asked.

"Revealed?" I said. "Oh, developed."

As soon as I said "developed," I wished I hadn't because it reminded me of our unit on puberty in school. I started blushing again. Besides, I like "revealed" more. I thought:

CAN A PHOTOGRAPH REVEAL
THE HAPPINESS I FEEL?

Miguel and I headed down the stairs and we all five reached the bottom at around the same time. Now that I think of it, I can't remember walking down. But obviously I must have—I couldn't have floated down!

At the bottom, we piled into our rented car and drove northeast to a tiny walled hilltop town. Pedraza (Pay Droth Ah, as Miguel says it) has no billboards or fast-food stores or *anything* modern.

We went to a restaurant that used to be the home of a painter named Zuloaga (Thoo Low Ah Ga). Mom had reserved a table on the upstairs glassed-in porch so that we could have a view of the countryside.

Matt said, "Where should I sit?"

Mom said, "Anywhere." I glanced at Miguel. He was looking at me, and without saying a word, he tilted his head toward one end of the table, and we took seats right next to each other. We did it quickly and quietly—as if we were playing musical chairs.

Outside the picture window was a tall old chimney covered with vines. On top of that was a nest or *nido* (Knee Dough), and on top of that was a duck. So I said, "*Pato*."

Miguel laughed. "Ducks do not build nests on chimneys, May Lah Nee. That is a stork."

"A stork?" Matt stood up.

"Are you sure?" It looked like a duck, sitting there all covered in white feathers.

"I assure you it is a stork," Miguel said. "That is true. But here is something that is not true: Storks bring babies—from Paris."

Paris! Home of French kissers!

"Storks bring babies in America too," Dad said. "But I have no idea where they get them."

"From a giant cabbage patch in the sky." Mom winked at me. She knows I know babies come from moms and dads, not storks and cabbages!

I took a photo of the stork just as it was standing up to stretch one of its long, skinny, unduck-like legs.

Outside, the clouds were growing grayer and grayer. Lines of lightning suddenly flashed and divided up the sky! It started to pour! But it wasn't rain—it was hail! Hailstones hurled themselves against the window.

PING! PING! PING!

Ten minutes later, the sky turned blue again. We even saw a rainbow in the distance.

I told Miguel that in New York, rainbows are unusual, and when you see one, you see just the top because skyscrapers get in the way. Here, the land stretches for miles (or kilometers!), and we could see the whole rainbow, from one end to the other.

"Rainbow" in Spanish is *arco iris* (R Co E Reese) or purple arch.

It was cool to watch the weather change. Now I'm wondering whether there's weather between people, and whether that weather changes. Usually between people, it's just regular air molecules. But between me and Miguel, before the storm, the air felt electric: charged up and changeable. And sometimes when he's close, it feels warm: pure sunshine. Other times, it's foggy—I can't tell what he's thinking. Other times, it's windy—as though I'm being pushed into him! After lunch today, it was all rainbows.

(I know that sounds dorky, but that's why I'm telling just you, my diary. Diaries never laugh or spread secrets!)

Well, while I was paying attention to all the indoor and outdoor weather, waiters brought out platters of roast lamb (*cordero* or Core Dare Oh) and suckling pig (*cochinillo* or Coach E Knee Yo). The suckling pig was an entire piglet on a plate, snout and all. I felt bad for it, but it was yummy and so tender that you didn't even need a knife to cut it. The lamb was *delicioso* too.

It was the best lunch I ever had. But maybe that's because Miguel was next to me, and I think he does like me—at least a little.

It feels pretty nice to feel pretty and nice!

After lunch, we walked around the narrow streets of Pedraza, and it started to rain again. Dad, Mom, and Matt started singing a song from *My Fair Lady:* "The rain in Spain stays mainly in the plain." That was embarrassing!

Miguel held his umbrella right over my head. That was romantic! I almost stepped in a puddle, and he sort of held my elbow and said, "*Cuidado*" (Quee Dodd Oh) or "Careful."

Wasn't that sweet?

Speaking of sweet, we went to another pastry shop and bought a ton of cookies for dessert. Matt went overboard, so I said, "He has a sweet tooth."

"A sweet tooth?" Miguel asked.

"It's an expression."

"Oh. Matt is like Cookie Monster on *Sesame Neighborhood.*"

Matt beamed and said, "Cooooooookie," then said, "It's *Sesame Street*, not *Sesame Neighborhood.*"

"Yes? We say *Sesame Neighborhood—Barrio Sésamo*" (Bah Rrree Oh Say Sah Mo).

"*Sesame Street* helped me learn the alphabet," I said.

"And how many letters are in the alphabet, Melanie?" Mom chimed in.

I thought, Weird question. But I said, "Twenty-six."

"You agree, Miguel?"

Miguel clicked his tongue, which is a Spanish way of saying no, and he and Mom explained that the Spanish alphabet has extra letters: rr (as in *barrio*), ll (as in *llama*), ñ (as in *mañana*), and ch (as in *chocolate*).

Here's another thing: Instead of calling w "double u," the Spanish call it "double v," which also makes sense, I guess.

Matt sneezed and Miguel said, "Hey Seuss," as though Dr. Seuss were his best buddy and he was calling him. But what he was actually saying was "*Jesús*," which is one Spanish way of saying "bless you."

To really learn a language, you have to learn so much more than vocabulary lists!

If you're wondering why I started out by saying that today was happy *and* sad, I will now get to the sad part.

We drove back to Madrid. Julio and Enrique Iglesias were singing mushy songs on the *radio* (Rah D O), and

Miguel was sitting next to me. We were very close to each other, but we were about to drop him off, and I realized that I will see him only once more before we go. And not for a whole day, just for a few *minutos* (Me New Toes).

Tomorrow my family is going to Seville, and in two days, we fly home from Madrid.

The good thing is: Miguel and his dad plan to say goodbye at the airport. They are flying to Valencia the same day we're flying to New York.

The bad thing is: Who wants to say goodbye?

GOODBYE—

Melanie the Windblown

P.S. Matt just said, "Knock, knock," so I said, "Who's there?"

He said, "Boo."

I said, "Boo who?"

He said, "Don't cry, Mellie, it's just a joke."

I said ha-ha-ha sarcastically, but all Matt did was smile.

March 26, 11ish

in a fast-fast-fast

Dear Diary,

we are on a modern train
Speeding to Seville, Spain!

The train we are on does not wait for anybody. It is called *AVE* (Ah Vay). That means bird, and it is *f-l-y-i-n-g*. *AVE* actually stands for *Alta Velocidad* (Ahl Ta Vay Low C Dodd), which means High Velocity, which means *f-a-s-t*. Dad said that if it arrives more than five minutes later than it's supposed to, you get your money back.

When Mom used to live here, it took forever to get from Madrid to southern Spain. We're doing it in under two and a half hours! Mom said it's a shame we won't get to see Granada and Cordoba, but Dad thinks it's great that we can whip down south and see Seville. (Dad probably also thinks it's great that it will finally be just us, the 4 M's.)

Matt talked me into playing Mad Libs.

I wonder what Miguel would think if he'd heard us.

When I asked Matt to give me verbs ending with *ing*, he offered "farting" and "burping." When I asked for nouns, he supplied "pee" and "boogie." When I needed adjectives, he came up with "blubbery" and "hairy." When I wanted a part of the body, he said "armpit" and "*culo*" (Coo Low).

"That's Spanish for 'butt,'" Matt explained. "Miguel taught me."

"Why'd he teach you that?"

"Because I asked."

Do all boys (even Miguel) have sick sides? I cannot picture Miguel putting his right hand under his left armpit and flapping to make farty noises.

But maybe Miguel can't picture me playing Bad Word Mad Libs!

"You know what else he taught me?"

"Who?" I inquired innocently.

"Miguel, duh!" Matt gave me a look as though *he* were the older sibling and *I* was the little idiot. "Remember when I sneezed yesterday and Miguel said, 'Hey Seuss'? Well, he asked me, 'Are you constipated?'

and I said, 'Huh?!' and we realized that *constipado* (Cone Stee Pa Doe) means having a stuffy nose even though 'constipated' means—"

"I know what it means, Matt."

He took the Mad Libs and started asking me for parts of speech. I provided interesting vocabulary words, such as "fretting," "excursion," and "windblown." When Matt asked for a place, instead of saying "bathroom," as he would have, I said "dark side of the moon," which I thought showed imagination. But at the end, Matt read the paragraph out loud, and it wasn't even half as funny as when he picks inappropriate words.

Which seemed unfair, really. I even mentioned this to Matt, and he said that if I'm too proper to use bad words, I could say "banana," "melons," or "lemons" because fruits are funny. I said I'd think about it.

Properly yours—
Mad Lib Mellie

@ 2.P.M. in a PARK

Dear Diary,

Seville is cool—but also hot! We are staying at the Hotel Murillo.

Mom wanted us to visit Murillo's house and go to a museum to see paintings by him and Zurbarán (Zoor Bah Ron). We said forget it. "What if I get you audio-guides?" Mom asked, but even she knew it was a lost cause.

"You go, Miranda," Dad said. "The kids and I will meet you at Columbus's tomb at four o'clock."

"Cool!" Matt said.

"Nothing's cool about today, Matt," said Dad. "It's hot as h-ll."

"Sure you don't want to come with me?" Mom said. "The museum will be air-conditioned. And nobody paints children as tenderly as Murillo—"

"I'm sick of art," Matt said. "I've seen enough tender babies and ugly ancestors."

"Matt, don't break your mother's heart," Dad said.

"Because then she'd be broken-arted?" He struck a stupid pose and said, "I could pose for Moo Ree Yo."

"No, you couldn't," Mom said. "He died in 1682."

"On Christmas?" Matt asked.

Mom looked exasperated. "I'll see you in a few hours."

"Buy a postcard of your favorite painting," I called after her. I was trying to be sensitive.

As soon as it was the three of us, Dad said, "Okay kids, what'll we do? It's so hot, you could fry an egg on the street."

"That's why some Spanish people take *siestas*," I said.

"Let's do it!" Matt said.

"Take a nap?" I said.

"Fry an egg!" Matt said.

"We don't have an egg," I said.

"We could buy an egg," Matt said.

"*Huevo*" (Way Vo), I said.

"I suppose we could," Dad said, which came as a shock.

Next thing you know, we were in a tiny grocery store buying one *huevo*, some sandwich stuff, and a kind of sliced Wonder bread called Bimbo (Matt said it must make you stupid instead of strong). The cashier barely noticed that we bought just one egg because it wasn't like in a supermarket where you have to buy an even number.

Matt said, "Now we have to find a place with no people around."

"Lead the way, champ," Dad said. You could tell Dad thought we were on quite the adventure. He's also much more relaxed now that he's on pure vacation.

Matt led us down twisting alleyways, and each one led to one more. It was like a giant maze. We passed whitewashed houses decorated with hanging flowerpots and peeked inside doorways to inner courtyards with pretty plants and trickling fountains.

"My turn to carry the egg," I said.

"Okay," Matt said. "But don't drop it. I get to drop it because it was my idea."

We walked some more until Matt found a sunny spot. I touched the pavement with my finger. It was as hot as beach sand in August.

"*Perfecto*" (Pair Fec Toe), I said. "Perfect."

"*Perfecto*," Dad repeated.

"Ready?" I handed Matt the egg.

"Think it will sizzle and fry?" he asked.

"Only one way to find out," Dad said.

Matt tossed the egg into the air. It went up, then down, then splatted into a nasty puddle.

We all watched. But nothing happened.

"Should I stir it?" Matt said.

"Be patient," I advised. "It might cook." The yolk oozed around. The egg insides mostly sat there, a gloppy Humpty Dumpty mess.

We kept watching and waiting, but the egg white didn't even turn white.

"I don't think it's going to fry," Dad said. "Shall we go?"

"We're just going to leave it?" Matt asked.

"You want to take it with you?" I asked. "Or eat it?"

"Let's wait a few more minutes," Matt pleaded, so we did.

The egg kind of disappeared into the street, leaving a see-through filmy surface with a pale white outline. The yolk part dried, thickened, and turned brownish-orange. Overall, though, it must not have been as hot as Dad had thought because what we were staring at was not a fried egg.

Even if you really try
You cannot force an egg to fry.
(I wonder if the fact above
Applies as well to things like love.)

"I guess we can leave," Matt said.

"That was highly educational," I said, because I didn't want Dad to regret letting us crack an egg in a foreign country. What I was thinking, though, was that yesterday at the castle was a lot more sizzling than our *experimento* (S Pair E Men Toe) in the alley.

We picnicked in a shaded area of a park called María Luisa (Ma Ree Ah Loo E Sa). Horse-drawn carriages clippity-clopped past, and black-and-white birds chirped and swooped, and cicadas hummed in the tall trees, announcing that it was hot hot hot—which we all knew anyway.

A brown-eyed girl approached us and held out her palm, asking for money. Dad said she was a Gypsy. She was around eight or nine, but her face seemed older and she wasn't playing, she was working. I felt bad for her because it's not her fault that her parents don't have any money, just as it's not thanks to me that my parents do have some. I reached into my pocket and gave her a euro, which is around a dollar. She said *gracias* and skipped away.

Pensively,
Melanie

Same day, almost 4:00 p.m.

next to Columbus's tomb in the third-biggest cathedral in Europe (after Rome's and London's)

Dear Diary,

The *Plaza de España* is full of colorful tiles of Spanish scenes. It is *muy* pretty. (Mooey means very.) It is also full of white doves. Matt chased them into the air even though it was too hot to run.

It was almost too hot to walk, but Dad made us walk to the cathedral. We didn't stop until we reached its courtyard of orange trees. I wish we had orange trees in New York. They smell so good—like springtime!

Matt wanted to climb the *Giralda* (Hhhee Rahl Da), so we did. It started out as a prayer tower with stone carved like lace and later became a bell tower with little balconies.

On top, there was an American girl with even more freckles than Matt. Matt and Freckle Girl started smiling at each other. A lot. They were looking down over Seville's orange trees and white houses and old bullring, and Matt told her all about Buddy and Ferdinand. She was hanging on his every word!

Is my brother a flirt? Should he be acting all smiley when he already has a girlfriend?

Then again, Lily must have friends who are boys, so maybe it's okay.

Since Matt was distracted, I asked Dad, "Were you worried about this trip?"

"Worried? Why?"

"About Mom."

"No. Think I should have been?"

"Well, you always say I worry too much, but—"

"Who? You? Mel-o-drama Mel?"

I made a face at him. "If I were you, I'd have worried." Dad smiled, so I added, "I'm serious."

"Okay, cupcake, I'll be serious too." He ruffled my hair. "Mom and I are well suited. We love each other and we love our 4-M Club. Was I as happy as she was about visiting Antonionio? No. But I didn't want to forbid it. Your mother likes to do things her way. And last year, she didn't mind when we had lunch with Sophia, remember?"

"She minded a little," I corrected him.

"Well, there you are. We don't always like it, but we try to respect each other, even when it's difficult."

"And that's when you have fights?"

Dad looked amused. "We do okay. And you know what, Melleroonie?"

"What?"

"Mom and Antonio broke up long ago. I wooed and won."

"Wooed?"

"Courted, dated, went out with."

I triiiiied to picture them wooing. I guess Dad is okay-looking (when he's not asleep). And he has a fun side (when he's not a grump). And he's smart and thoughtful (most of the time).

"Dad," I said, "no one says 'wooed' anymore. 'Wooed' is a weird word."

"Not weally," he replied, so I poked him. He poked me back. Then he called over to Matt. "Let's go. Let's rock 'n' roll."

"No one says that anymore either," I pointed out.

Dad laughed. "I do."

We are now inside the big cathedral, waiting for Mom. It's dark and cool—naturally cool, not air-conditioned cool. We got here early, but I didn't mind because I wanted to write.

Right next to me are statues of four Spanish kings with crowns. They are carrying Columbus's coffin!

I can't believe I am two yards away from whatever is left of Columbus! "Columbus is in there—but dead?" Matt asked.

"According to this guidebook," Dad said.

"It must be mostly Columbus dust," I said.

"And bone bits," Matt added.

Matt and I walked around the coffin twice.

"I wish we could tell him the good news—that he found a whole new continent," I said.

"I'm going to!" Matt said. He faced the coffin and whispered, "Hey, Columbus! Way to go! You didn't find Asia, but you did discover *America*. And you're still famous!"

Dad said, "Want to give Chris some bad news too?"

"What do you mean?" I asked.

"His discoveries were great for Spain but not so great for the people on the islands where he landed because he brought germs and diseases with him."

"On purpose?" Matt asked.

"No, not on purpose!" Dad said.

"What diseases?" I asked.

"Smallpox and measles, for starters. It wiped out a lot of the native population."

"Like a plague?" I asked.

"I'm afraid so," Dad said.

When Dad wasn't looking, I whispered to the coffin, "That wasn't really your fault."

Dad said that Columbus kept a diary—like me. But guess what? He kept *two* ship logs. In the public one his sailors saw, he wrote things like *We've sailed a short way and we're getting there*. In the private one he kept just for himself, he wrote things like *We've been at sea a long long long time—I'm worried. Where the heck is land?!* Nobody had thought it would take over a month to get from one shore to the next, and Columbus didn't want to stress anyone out.

Too late! His crew was already going crazy!

"After thirty days at sea," Dad said, "some sailors begged Columbus to turn around and go home. Some even plotted to throw him overboard and sail back! But he convinced them to hang in there a little longer. And then, just in time—"

"Land ho!!!" Matt cried out.

"Exactly," Dad said, "but shhh, we're in a cathedral."

Three wooden ships rocked to and fro.
The crew's morale was very low.
Things looked bleak, but next thing you know—
The crow's-nest man called out: "LAND HO!"

Actually, in Spanish, "Land ho!" is "*¡Tierra!*" (Tyair Ah). And Christopher Columbus is Cristobal Colón (Cree Sto Ball Co Loan). Sounds like Crystal Ball Cologne.

If I had a crystal ball, I would look into it and see what Miguel is doing, then look further to see us saying goodbye, then peer way into the future to find out if we'll ever see each other again.

I hope Mom gets here soon because even though I usually like thinking about Miguel, I also like living in the present and knowing that I can still think about everything else in the world.

It *is* a big world! And a round one!

Warmly,

Melanie ←the world!

P.S. "World" in Spanish is *mundo* (Moon Dough).

8:30 p.m. in our Seville hotel

Dear Diary,

King Peter the Cruel (who must not have been very nice) built palaces called the *Reales Alcázares* (Ray Ahl S Ahl Ca Sar S). They are part Muslim, part Christian, and very old.

We visited them, and in the Garden of the Poets, it was quiet, so I closed my eyes and tried to think poetic thoughts. But Matt bounded over, blocked my sun, and said, "Doesn't this remind you of *Aladdin*? You be Jasmine and I'll be Aladdin!"

His voice sounded like the stop-start whine of a *mosquito* (Mo Ski Toe).

"I have a better idea," I said. "*You* be Aladdin. Now go take a flying carpet ride!"

"You're no fun."

"Yes, I am. But I want to be alone for two seconds. Is that too much to ask?" It's not easy to get any privacy on a family vacation.

"Well, I'm bored."

"And that's *my* problem?"

"C'mon, Mellie. I helped you have a private rowboat ride."

He was right. He did. And so for the next hour, he was Aladdin and I was Jasmine, and we ran around the palace and through a maze of tall hedges.

Mom overheard us playing and I could tell she appreciated my being a P.B.S.—Perfect Big Sister. "Having fun?" she asked.

"Not really. I'm *caliente*" (Ca Lee N Tay).

"Careful, pumpkin. 'I'm hot,' in Spanish has a different meaning than in English. It means 'I'm a hottie' or 'I'm sexy' or—"

"I get it!" I shouted so she wouldn't keep explaining. I was about to stick my fingers in my ears and go be-be-be-be-be but she stopped. I'm just relieved that I didn't tell Miguel I was a hottie!!

"Instead of 'I am hot,'" Mom said, "Spaniards say, 'I have heat'—'*Tengo calor*'" (Tang O Ca Lore).

Dad came over and Mom asked, "Ready to go to the Museum of Archaeology?"

Matt objected. "You said no more museums!"

Mom said, "I said, 'No more *art* museums.' That's not an art museum."

"What?" Matt said.

"That's so not fair!" I said.

"We'll go for just half an hour and then we'll get ice cream—*helado*," Mom said, bribing us. Ay Lah Doe actually means "frozen."

"There better be benches!" Matt grumbled.

There were. There was also something shocking. Matt and I were playing our favorite museum game when we came across a statue of a naked person. We're totally used to that, but this naked person had developed in a boy way *and* a girl way! The statue was sort of a man with bosoms—or a lady with a you-know-what.

We showed Mom. "Fascinating," she said, and read the label underneath. "A hermaphrodite." Mom was acting as if this were just another statue, no big deal, but Aladdin Boy couldn't get over its being right there in public. (I couldn't either.)

Mom and Dad were holding hands, and Dad was saying that Spain was ruled by Romans for hundreds of years, and by Moors for hundreds of years. I could feel a history lecture coming on, and the thirty minutes were definitely up, so I said, "Who wants *helado*?"

MOM took her cue
And she said, "ME!"
MATT said, "ME TOO!"
DAD said, "ME THREE!"
So that Mu-se-o
Was his-tor-y!

I ate my ice cream cone the normal way, Matt ate his from the bottom up, and we walked though the alleyways to our hotel. In our room, Matt and I played Towel Bullfight. I have improved my technique and am a better matador than before. Bull Boy, however, still just snorts and charges around, as demented as ever.

I hope we have dinner soon because that cone did not hold me. Spaniards eat late but my stomach is from New York!

Ravenously yours,

MELANIE

back at the Oh Tell

Dear Diary,

Dinner was embarrassing and I will tell you why.

Seville is full of restaurants with outside tables, so we ate outside. Mom and Dad had fried fish, Matt and I had paella, and we all tried *gazpacho* (Gahs Pa Cho), which is a cold bumpy soup. You make it by putting bread, tomatoes, peppers, and other veggies in a blender with spices. On top, you can sprinkle chopped-up cucumber and onion. It's like liquid salad and it's good for you. Problem is, it tastes gross. (Dad disagreed. He lapped mine up.)

But that was not what was embarrassing. What was embarrassing was that Mom and Dad also had a wine punch called *sangría* (Sahn Gree Ah). The ingredients are wine, seltzer, sugar, cinnamon, sliced oranges, lemons, and apples. (Mostly wine.)

I said, "Sangria is *not* for parents on vacation with kids."

Dad laughed. "Mellie, that's precisely who it *is* for!"

They split an entire jug! Mom could tell I was looking at her funny, so she said, "Honey, tomorrow is our anniversary." (As though that is an excuse to drink in front of your children!) Instead of talking about Columbus or whatever, Dad was telling Mom about, as he put it, our eggcellent egg eggsperiment. He must have been telling it eggstra funny because Mom was laughing until she had tears in her eyes.

And then she started singing!!

In Spanish!!!

She also started clapping her hands in the air like a Spanish dancer. She was acting like a teenager! Dad didn't mind—maybe he even enjoyed imagining Mom as a student in Spain. I told her to keep it down, and I told myself that at least no one *I* knew was going to walk by.

I have to admit, the song was pretty. Also bittersweet (one of my favorite compound words).

The first line sounds like this: No Tay Vy Oss Toe Da V Ah, but I'm about to ask Mom to write it down in Spanish. Here comes Mom's handwriting:

No te vayas todavía,
No te vayas por favor,
No te vayas todavía
Que hasta la guitarra mía llora
Cuando dice adiós.

The translation is sad sad sad. It's

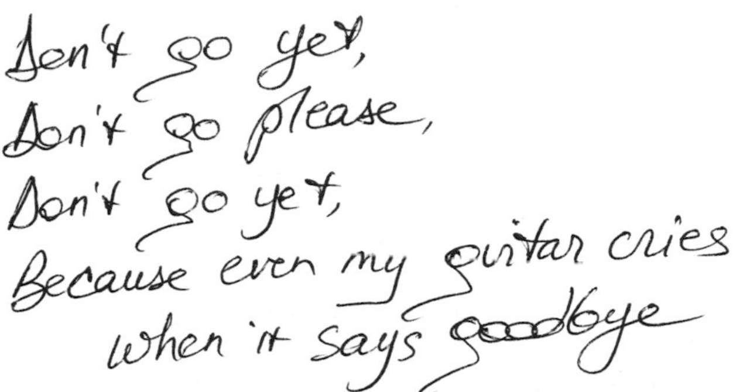

I am going to say goodbye to you now, goodbye to Seville tomorrow, and goodbye to Spain—and Miguel—the day after that.

Bye with a sigh—
Melanie Martin, Goodbye Girl

March 27, not quite 10 A.M.
at our hotel in Seville

Dear Diary,

Guess what we did this morning?

Slept in! Last night Mom and Dad had said they wanted to take it easy and not to come to their room before 10:30.

Our room has a tiny terrace and if you step out, you can see the *Giralda*. You can hear its bells too!

I wrote a poem:

Seville is on a river
Called the Guadalquivir.
We smelled orange trees in bloom
And saw Columbus's tomb.
We helped a girl who was a Gypsy,
And Mom got a little tipsy.

I don't know whether to show it to Mom or not.

Probably not.

Matt and I are about to make an anniversary card for Mom and Dad. Fourteen years is a lot!

Happy March 27th
Melanie

early afternoon

in a bar (even though that sounds strange)

Dear Diary,

Mom and Dad loved our homemade card.

It said, "We are glad you got married and had us. You are the best parents ever! Love, Melanie and Matt." It took us over an hour to make. On it we doodled a map of Spain, a bull, a paella, fireworks, an iguana, a half fish, a Picasso-y painting, that blond Velázquez girl, the five-legged horse, the aqueduct, a castle, orange trees, and bunches of hearts. (Matt wanted to draw the shocking statue but I said no.)

Breakfast was *churros* (Chew Rrrose), which are strips of fried dough. Matt and I ate ours with yummy hot *chocolate* that was so thick, it looked like dark brown Elmer's glue.

Then Dad got a haircut. Why? Well, *The Barber of Seville* is the opera with the famous "Figaro Figaro Figaro" song, and Mom thought it would be funny if Dad went to "see" a barber in Seville. Get it? Matt went too. Not me—I like my hair long! And not Mom—she'd just gotten her hair cut (so she could look nice for Antonionio).

Speaking of opera, Dad once took me to an opera called *Carmen*. It's also set in Seville. It's about a beautiful Gypsy lady who works in a cigarette factory—yuck! She sings her lungs out about how "love is like a wild bird" and throws a red flower at a man, José, who falls right in love with her. But Carmen is *not* a one-man woman and she starts liking a bullfighter too. José gets jealous, Carmen dumps him, and he stabs her to death outside a bullring.

The story is violent. But the music is catchy.

Last month, Mom was reading the section in her college magazine where everyone brags about what they've been up to since graduation. Well, Mom read about a classmate who lives in Seville whose daughter takes flamenco dance lessons. Mom e-mailed the guy, and he arranged for us to go to a class. All we had to do was promise to be quiet.

So today we went to a Flamenco Foundation and got to see a real flamenco dance class! Even Matt liked it. I wish Cecily could have seen it because she takes ballet in New York.

The teacher's name was María José (Ma Ree Ah Hhho Say), which would sound strange in English. After all, it combines a lady's name (Mary) with a man's name (Joseph), and it seems religious.

She did a lot of clapping. Not like "Good job, children" clapping, more like clapping to help the kids keep time and pay attention to when to stomp their feet and twirl their hands and swish their skirts.

Most of the students were my age or younger. They wore crisp white shirts and long flowy skirts and black high heels. Mom's classmate's daughter was soooo cute. She kept stomping her foot as loudly as she could, but it was never *that* loud because she is not that big.

If I took flamenco and practiced stomping at home, my feet would get sore and my downstairs neighbor would have a cow or *vaca* (Ba Ca).

A different girl, Matt's age, was looking at Matt and

smiling just like the American girl he met yesterday with the connect-the-dots face. Matt smiled back!

Is he Mr. Friendly? Or a Junior Don Juan??

The Gypsy music played, and María José corrected the girls on how to stand proud and click their wooden castanets—the small round instruments they held in each hand. She taught them fancy footwork or *zapateado* (Sop Ah Tay Ah Dough), arm movements or *braseo* (Bra Say Oh), and hand motions or *flore* (Floor Ay). The girl Matt's age was practicing eye movements too—she kept looking at Matt!

By the end of the class, the girls were sweating.

We thanked them, and Matt looked at the girl and pointed at himself and said Ma Tay Oh. She pointed to herself and said Tay Race Ah. Then he said, "*Adiós*, Teresa." After that, I doubt Matt even thought about her, but for all I know, she ran home to write all about Ma Tay Oh the Brat Ay Oh in her diary.

Right now, we 4-M's are having a stand-up lunch. Dad said he wanted to go to a *tapas* (Top Ahs) bar. I said, "A topless bar?" but Mom reminded me that *tapas* are appetizers or little bites to eat. You'd think Mom and Dad would have wanted a fancy sit-down anniversary lunch, but they love *tapas*.

They ordered mushrooms, mussels, minnows, and meatballs. (Thank heavens for meatballs.) Mom usually asks for things in Spanish, but Dad checks out the food on the counter and points to whatever looks good. They wanted me to try mussels, and I said, "I will when I'm older." (I wonder how long I'll be able to get away with saying that.)

Matt kept asking for more meatballs. He says food tastes better on toothpicks, same as drinks taste better through straws. He even told Mom and Dad, "If you ever want us to eat leftovers, serve them on toothpicks."

Dad said they have a surprise lined up for us.

"A present?" Matt said.

"An experience," Mom said, and she and Dad looked at each other all mysteriously.

I hope it's fun!

Crossing my fingers

Martin Melanie

P.S. I wrote my last name first because my gersfin were crossed!

midnight in the hotel

Dear Diary,

"The kids will never forget this," Dad said, and he may be right.

We just came back from a flamenco show. Not a class. A *show*!

It's now midnight and Mom told us to get in our pajamas or *pijamas* (Pea Hhhom Ahs). So I did.

Right now, even as I write, Matt is clapping and stomping around our hotel room, pretending to be a Gypsy or *gitano* (Hhhe Tahn Oh). He looks half cute, half dorky. He's singing too, but he sounds like a wolf howling. Or ululating (is that how you spell it??).

I took two photos and was tempted to tell Matt that I was going to send them to Freckle Girl and Flamenco Girl. (Hee, hee.) But he knew I didn't have their addresses.

I think Matt and I appreciated tonight's show extra because we'd seen how hard flamenco dancing is to learn. I wonder if kids who take music lessons appreciate concerts extra.

While we were waiting for the show to begin, Dad had said, "Flamenco is as Spanish as bullfighting."

"Without the death part," I pointed out.

"It's about life," Mom agreed. "Living it and feeling it. That's very Spanish." She told us about another experience that is very *español:* the running of the bulls. Every year on July 7, Spaniards and tourists go running through the streets of Pamplona with real bulls chasing after them. Every year people get hurt, but they keep doing it.

"That's *loco*," I said.

"Not on my to-do list," Mom agreed.

Dad said, "Shhh," because four men came out wearing black shirts and black pants. One was playing a guitar and the other three were kind of clapping. "They're not exactly clapping," Dad explained. "They're playing their hands the way other people play an instrument." It's called *tocar palmas* (Toe Car Palm Ahs) or playing palms.

"Where are the ladies in the polka-dotted dresses?" Matt asked.

Right on cue, out came four women in bright floor-length puffed-out dresses with layers of ruffles. One dress was flamingo pink with black polka dots. Another was blood red with no dots. A third was sky blue with white dots. A fourth was lemon yellow with green dots.

Spotlights followed them around.

The women wore red lipstick, thick eye makeup, and hoop earrings. Their black hair was clipped back in buns and stuck with flowers.

You know how ballet dancers are usually skinny? Well, these dancers weren't. Mom called them "full-figured—more hourglass than toothpick." Dad said they were "sexy"! (Mom jabbed him—after all, it *is* their anniversary.)

You know how ballet dancers dance delicately on tiptoe? Well, these dancers do the opposite. They land hard on their heels. Sometimes they bang their feet down, step around softly, then bang them down again.

Flamenco dancing is not like tap dancing either. Tap dancers smile. Flamenco dancers are serious.

Loud too! The dancers' hands and feet filled the room with sound. And sometimes they clicked their castanets furiously. It made me think of drumming. Or of the *Mascletà* of firecrackers.

Spaniards in the audience were saying *olé* just like at the bullfight. So we did too!

The eight Gypsies took turns dancing and clapping. Dad said one man had "lightning legs."

While one of the men was pounding the floor, one of the women lifted her dress a little so we could see her stomp-stomp-stomping back. It was like an intense movie that you couldn't turn away from even if you wanted to. The woman was looking into the man's eyes and snapping her fan open and shut. It was like flirting, but it wasn't sweet or shy. It was fierce and powerful, as though she and he were having a stare-down and daring each other about something.

The Gypsies were taking turns singing too. The songs were low and sad and you didn't have to understand the words to tell that they were about love and longing and that someone's feelings had gotten hurt. Maybe even stomped on!

One Gypsy sounded as if he wasn't singing, he was moaning. It was beautiful but sorrowful or, as Mom said, "soulful."

She translated what he sang:

"She left me and I loved her;
there will never be another. . . ."

I listened to the singing and guitar playing, and I watched the Gypsies and their dancing shadows on the wall. It was pretty sizzling!

A man and a woman got so so so close to each other that I wanted them to go ahead and kiss behind her opening and closing fan. And that made me think about getting a little closer to Miguel. But then a different man and woman danced so gloomily and tragically that I started worrying that I might already be in over my head. And that made me think that I should run for cover before I end up learning about the crushing part of having a crush.

The pain and jealousy and heartache and heartbreak.

Here in the hotel, Matt is being funny/gross. He is clapping and stomping, and in a low trembly flamenco-y voice, he's been singing, "I am brokenhearted." Well, he just blew into his arm and made a disgusting sound, and added, "I'm also broken-farted."

Mom and Dad have now come back into our room.

"Matt!" Mom scolded. "What did I ask you to do?"

"Get in my pajamas," Matt replied. "My Peeeeee Hhhom Ahs."

"And what have you been doing all this time?" Mom said.

"Singing and dancing," Matt said.

Did Mom yell at him? No. She gave him a hug and said, "Oh, Matt, you are hard to get mad at."

"I know," he said, and smiled. (He gets away with everything!)

Mom and Dad kissed us good night, and Mom even tucked in Hedgehog, Flappy Happy, and the Iggies.

After Mom and Dad left, Matt asked, "Can I write in your diary?"

"Of course not," I said.

"Pleeeeease."

"No way!"

"Just one word."

I figured it would be faster to let him write one word than to keep arguing so I said, "Fine, but just one and nothing gross."

He said it wouldn't be but I'd have to help him spell it.

I said okay and I am now handing Matt my diary. Here comes Matt's handwriting:

Polkadot

"Polka dot"? I don't know what I was expecting. "Boob"? "Butt"? "Boogie"?

I told Matt that "polka dot" is two words, not one, but he said he hadn't known. "So you can't get mad at me."

I said, "I could if I felt like it!"

Well, tomorrow is a travel day: first train, then plane. It's also when I'll see Miguel Miguel Miguel!

Happily yours—

Melanie Melanie Melanie

P.S. Last-minute inspiration:

Did we see any polka dots?

Yes! Lots and lots and lots and lots!

March 28

morning in the train

Dear Diary,

This morning Mom and Dad said we could pick out a Spanish souvenir. Mom offered me a polka-dotted ruffly dress, but I couldn't picture myself wearing it. She also offered castanets or a ceramic plate or blue-and-white tile, but I said no thanks. That's when Matt spotted a store that makes posters. He chose a bullfight poster, and a man wrote Matt's name in block letters on it as though he were an ear-winning matador. I chose a poster with a beautiful flamenco dancer on it, but Dad said I had to pick the bullfight one too.

I started getting mad, but Dad said, "Relax, I'm pulling your leg."

"Don't!" I said, and Mom told us that in Spanish, teasing isn't "pulling your leg," it's "pulling your hair" or *tomando el pelo* (Toe Mahn Dough L Pay Low), which makes even more sense.

I asked the man to write MELANIE MARTIN on my poster so it would seem as if I were a *famosa* dancer. It didn't take long, and now Matt and I have bedroom posters and Mom has a classroom poster.

Our posters are so cool—and so Spanish. In some ways, the Gypsy and the matador are both saying, "Live your life! Be aware that you're alive!"

We are now speeeeeeeding back to Madrid.

I am aware of olive trees and grazing sheep and dark tunnels.

Dad began reading *Don Quixote*, which is the fat funny book Miguel mentioned. Dad said Cervantes and Shakespeare both died in 1616.

I said, "1616 was a sad year for writing."

Don Quixote loved stories about knights in shining armor so much that he started thinking of himself as a heroic knight on a great adventure. But really he was just an almost fifty-year-old on a worn-down horse with a roly-poly friend on a dumpy donkey.

Dad kept laughing, so Matt asked, "What's so funny?"

Dad said, "Don Quixote was really into books, okay? Well, listen to this: 'From so little sleeping and so much reading, his brains dried up and he lost his mind.'"

"Where does it say that?" Matt asked. Dad pointed.

"Could that happen?" I asked.

"Of course not," Mom said. "There's no such thing as reading too much—or writing too much."

Guess who else is on this train? Freckle Girl! She walked by our seats and Matt got up to sit with her. I whispered, "What about Lily?"

"What about her?" He looked at me as if I'd drunk too much sangria. "There's no law that says you can't talk to people."

He's probably right. But how did my little brother get so comfortable with boy-girl stuff?

Off he went, while here I sit, not even sure whether the glow between Miguel and me means anything or not.

Since Dad is reading and Matt's gone, Mom started singing again, but softly and just for me. She sang, "Madrid, Madrid, Madrid, *pedazo de la España en que nací*" (Pay Da So Day La S Pon Ya N K Na C), which means "piece of Spain where I was born." She thought I'd like it because it repeats Madrid three times.

Mom knows me well well well.

afternoon at the airport

or *aeropuerto* (Air O Pwair Toe)

Dear Diary,

We took a bus from the train station to the airport and we've checked our stuff and are ready to fly home.

Just two things left to do:

1. Say *adiós* to Miguel and Antonio (they're supposed to be here), and

2. Get on the plane or *avión* (Ah V Own).

My stomach is flip-flopping. I could say it's fear of flying, but that's not it. I'm anxious about seeing Miguel. I wish it could be the two of us (not the whole family), and for a few hours (not a few minutes), and to say hello (not goodbye).

Heading Home,

Melanie

a little later

Dear Dear Dear Diary,

I will never forget today as long as I live.

Miguel and Antonio got to the airport just fifteen minutes before they had to board their flight to Valencia. Antonio offered to take a photo of us four, so we let him, but instead of smiling, we all decided to frown because leaving stinks.

Miguel said, "Matt, I have a present for you."

"You do?" Matt said, cheering right up.

Miguel handed Matt a black bull. It was so cute that I couldn't help feeling jealous. It has white horns and a red tongue and a long tail and a wind-up knob that makes its tail go round and round.

"That's *adorable*" (Odd Or Ob Lay), I said.

Then Miguel told his dad he wanted to show me something in a nearby store. Antonio looked at his watch and said, "Okay, but come right back. Be rapid."

"*Rápido*" (Rrrah Pee Dough), Mom said, looking at me. "Make it quick."

I followed Miguel a short distance down the airport

hallway and we stepped behind a wall. People hurried by, but it felt as if we were alone.

"May Lah Nee, I am glad you came to Spain."

"Me too." He looked even cuter than he did when I first met him. He reached for my hand. He didn't really hold it, though; he sort of laced his fingers through my fingers. I added, "But I'm a little sad to say goodbye." The word "goodbye" came out wobbly.

Miguel smiled a sweet smile. "Then don't say *adiós*, May Lah Nee. Say '*Hasta la próxima*' "(Ah Sta La Proke C Ma). I must have looked confused because he said, "That means, 'Until next time.' We will see each other again, yes?"

I nodded. I was afraid to actually speak because if I did, I knew I might cry. All of a sudden, two tears started in my eyes anyway and wet my lashes and drip-dropped onto my cheeks. I hoped Miguel wouldn't notice, but of course he did.

He touched my two cheeks with his two thumbs and wiped the tears away. It was embarrassing, but also, somehow, romantic and sweet and okay.

He handed me a tiny box and said, "Open it."

I undid the bow and ripped off the paper and lifted the lid and picked up the cotton.

And there was a necklace! A silvery chain with a little Spanish fan. It was shiny and delicate and lovely.

I said *gracias*, but I think my eyes said more.

He picked up the necklace. "You permit me?"

I nodded and he put the necklace on me. "Beautiful," he said.

"Miguel?"

"*¿Sí, señorita?*"

"Do you have e-mail?"

"Electronic mail? Yes." He smiled. Then he smoothed back a strand of my hair and cupped my chin and sort of tilted my face up toward his. I was looking into his eyes and I didn't want to break away. Ever! But he closed his eyes for just a half second, and leaned forward a tiny bit, and put his lips gently on my forehead, and he . . . kissed me.

MY FIRST KISS!
MY FIRST KISS!!
MY FIRST KISS!!!

I know Spaniards kiss each other on the cheek all day long (believe me, I *know* this), but I hadn't seen anyone kiss anyone else on the forehead. So I know it meant something.

I think I even know what.

I didn't kiss back, but I smiled back and said, "I will write you."

"And I will write you."

We gave each other our e-mail addresses. I was half tempted to say, "Pinky swear?" but I didn't think I needed to.

We joined the others, and Antonio air-kissed Matt and me and shook Dad's hand and hugged Mom goodbye. It wasn't a clap-on-the-back hug. It was a real hug, but a brief one.

After Antonio and Miguel left (we said goodbye again with our eyes), I wondered if my family could tell anything was different. I doubt I looked different except for the necklace, and it was hidden inside my shirt.

I feel a little different, though: older or taller or calmer or something. And my stomach isn't doing flip-flops anymore. It's almost as if I have a toasty warm bonfire inside me now, not big and out of control, but not tiny and going out either. It feels . . . just right.

With Love From Spain,
Melanie Martin

P.S. Some girls might not consider my first kiss a first kiss since it wasn't on the lips. But I think it counts way more than a spin-the-bottle kiss because it was full of feelings.

Dear Diary, STILL IN THE *aeropuerto*

Guess what? Our flight was overbooked, so the airline people had to find passengers willing to give up their seats and leave tomorrow instead of today. We still have four days before school starts, so Mom and Dad started talking fast and Dad checked his Thursday schedule to see if he had any urgent meetings tomorrow that are unpostponable (which I doubt is a word). He didn't. An *azafata* said, "We need four more volunteers," and said if someone volunteered to be "bumped," that person would be put up in a hotel and "sent out tomorrow on the next available flight to their final destination" and (this is the best part) would get free round-trip tickets to Europe valid for one year.

Mom could *not* stand it anymore. She shouted, "We volunteer!"

Get this: The airline thanked us! Mom said we should have thanked them!

Fortunately, I packed Hedgehog and you in my airplane bag.

Unfortunately, the rest of our luggage was already

checked, and because of security, they took it off the original plane, so we can't get it until we're in New York. Instead, they gave us each a little overnight travel bag of "toiletries" (Matt's new favorite word).

Well, the airlines do not care if you're a boy or a girl (or both!), they give the same bag to everybody. Here's what's in it: an extra-large white T-shirt for sleeping; big black socks; a toothbrush with a tiny tube of toothpaste; a razor; shaving cream (!); feminine pads (!); teeny bottles of detergent, moisturizer, shampoo, and body wash; a small deodorant; tissues; and a comb.

Mom said this is all part of our *aventura*.

I said that we will look funny in the airport hotel with our matching T-shirts. Dad's and Mom's might fit okay, but Matt and I are going to look like ghosties.

BOO—

Mel

P.S. I still can't believe the <u>other</u> thing that happened today!

Dear Diary,

None of us minded having an extra evening in Spain because we all like Spain. Mom even got to race alone through a hard-to-pronounce museum near the Prado. We kids refused to go, so Dad stayed with us, but he did give Matt and me each a business card from the hotel just in case we got lost or *perdido* (Pair D Dough). In Spanish, of course, if two people get lost, they get losts or *perdidos* (Pair D Dose)!

Anyway, later, when Mom met up with us, we said, "Close your eyes!" Matt took one of her hands and I took the other and we led her to a place called the *Museo del Jamón* (Moo Say Oh Del Hhhahm Own) or Ham Museum. It's actually a bar with hhhundreds of hhhams hhhanging by their hhhooves—from the ceiling. They look like dark pink chandeliers. We figured Mom would think it was funny that *we* took *her* to a museum.

And she did! She even raised her glass of wine and said a famous Spanish toast to us. Here is the translation: "Love, health, money, and time to enjoy them."

Since it was my last evening in Spain, I tried to be extra observant.

You know how you have five senses? Not *you*, Diary, I mean people. Not to rub it in or anything, but I assume you can't see or hear or taste or smell or feel. Not the way people can anyway. Or maybe you can feel? Can you feel me writing in you right now? Does it tickle?

Whoa—I must be in a really weird mood!! Good thing diaries are private!!

What I wanted to say is that we all have five senses, but sometimes we use some of them more than others. Like Mom uses mostly her eyes in museums. And Dad uses mostly his ears at the opera. And we all used our eyes and ears at the flamenco show. Well, in Spain, I think my sense of smell has been paying extra attention. I've been smelling open fires, salty air, orange trees, and lots of delicious garlic sizzling in olive oil.

Funny thing is, I didn't think I even liked garlic.

The other sense I have been extra aware of is touch. I can still almost feel Miguel's fingers in my fingers and hand on my chin and lips on my forehead.

Who knows? Maybe I'm more aware of *all* my feelings—of being alive.

Well, our airline hotel ran out of four-person rooms and adjoining rooms, so Dad and Matt took one room and Mom and I took another. Dad said, "Male bonding," and Mom said, "Female bonding."

To tell you the truth, which I obviously do anyway, Matt and I like when we get to sleep by our parents even though it's not something we go around admitting.

I am hereby admitting that it was fun to female-bond with Mom.

Right now, she is reading. She's using a Murillo postcard as a bookmark. It's of a mother and child.

I think Mom wanted to talk because she asked, "Did you and Miguel get a chance to say a nice goodbye?"

"A really nice goodbye." I tried not to have a goofy smile.

"I'm glad for you and for him," she said. "I'm even glad for Antonio because it's a blessing to have a good kid." She squeezed my hand.

"I'm a kid, but in less than two years, I'll be a teenager."

"True, but enjoy these years. Don't wish them away."

"Do you think I'll see Miguel again?"

"Would you like to?"

"*Sí.*"

"Then I think you will, though maybe not very soon."

"We'll e-mail."

"What a nice idea. Maybe in Spanish and English." (Leave it to Teacher Mom to think of love letters as educational.)

"But what if I don't see him again?" I asked. "And what if I never meet anyone else I like as much?" My dumb voice started wobbling—which I had not expected. "I mean, I already miss him and we haven't even left Spain! Will I get totally miserable and heartbroken like the Gypsy dancers?"

"No, honey bun, you won't."

"How do you know?"

"I know."

For some reason, maybe because Cecily wasn't there to talk to, I showed Mom my necklace.

"I was going to ask," she said. "It's very pretty."

I told her about my first *beso* too. Mom didn't seem toooo shocked, but then, it's not as if I was describing an R-rated make-out scene.

"So that must mean he likes me, right? I mean, like-likes me."

"Sounds like a reasonable assumption," Mom said. "Besides, he's smart. And you're likeable." She touched the little fan around my neck. "But you know what, pumpkin? He's the first boy you've felt this way about, not the last. And that was your first kiss, not your last—though as your mom, I hope you'll take your sweet time on all this. Your second kiss may be a long way off. And you're way too young for serious kissing."

"My first kiss was a serious kiss."

"True. But you know what I mean."

I had to admit that I did. "Do you think it was love?"

"Love?" Mom held the word in her mouth as though it were an M&M. "You know what a poet named Pablo Neruda wrote about love?"

"No."

"'Love is so short and forgetting is so long.'" She stared into space for a second.

"So was it love?" I asked. "Is it?"

"'Love' is a very big word," Mom said. "I think it was *lovely*—is lovely."

"And you don't think I'll get lovesick—and lovelorn?"

"I think you'll get busy with school and friends and activities. And I think you'll check your e-mail more than ever." She wiggled my big toe as though I were five. "I also think this is a colorful chapter in the book of your life." I didn't say anything, so Mom continued. "But you know who is the main character of your life?"

"Who?"

"You! And you're just eleven, so keep ahold of that big heart of yours, okay?"

I said okay in Spanish, which is *vale* (Ba Lay). Then I said, "You know how you said there are many different kinds of love?"

"Yes."

"Well, I think there are many different kinds of kisses too." I was thinking about single kisses, double kisses, cheek kisses, lip kisses, little bird kisses, spin-the-bottle kisses, even forehead kisses.

Mom kissed me. "I think you're right, precious."

"What about you and Antonio?" I said. "Did you get to say a nice goodbye?" It seemed only fair to ask.

"You were all there to witness it!" Mom smiled. "Yes, it was a nice goodbye. It was wonderful to see him again."

"Wonderful?" I like mom-daughter girl talk, but I was hoping Mom wasn't going to confide that she was thinking of using her free ticket for a one-way trip back to Spain.

"Mellie, he wasn't just my boyfriend a long time ago, he was also my friend. To never see him again would have been a shame. Of course, it also would have been bad if we'd seen each other and thought we were awful, or if we had not been able to speak each other's language, or if we'd started wishing we'd never broken up in the first place. But none of that happened. Seeing Antonio just felt good and somehow *settling*. Now I'm hoping Antonio and his wife get back together—and from what he told me, it sounds like they might. I bet she's a nice woman because she's the mother of a nice boy, right?"

"Right."

"And because, after all, Antonio has always had excellent taste in women. Like father, like son, right?"

"Right," I repeated.

"To be honest, during all those years when I hadn't seen Antonio, he was still sort of there in the very distant background, like that fifth leg in the painting. That ghost leg?"

"Pentimento," I said.

"Exactly." Mom smiled. "I think that if someone makes it all the way into your heart, that person stays with you forever—one way or another, mostly for better and occasionally for worse. A past love is part of the big picture of your life. Dad would say the same thing—he and Sophia were happy to see each other again in Rome, remember? So when that poet wrote that forgetting is so long, maybe it's because some of us never do forget. Maybe we don't even want to."

"Do you think Miguel and I will remember each other forever even if we never see each other again?"

"I think so, yes." I could tell Mom was really trying to get this right. "But just because an old sweetheart gets to have a little corner of your heart doesn't mean he or she gets to take up the whole space."

"But at least it won't be like it never happened." My stupid untrustworthy voice got all high and quivery again.

"Don't worry, honey. People remember their first kisses—and yours was very special." I halfway nodded. "You know how I like visiting paintings? Well, you can visit your memories. Everyone can. Experience stays with you. Memories last. They may fade but they never really go away."

Maybe Mom's right. Like when people go to a lot of trouble to make a Thanksgiving turkey and it gets gobbled right up, or when people go to a lot of trouble to make a *falla* and it gets burned right down. It's not a waste or as if it never happened because everyone remembers it. Forever.

I was still wishing I had more of Miguel than memories when I realized that I do. I have the necklace. And soon I'll have photos.

"Melanie, you and Miguel will always remember each other, at least in a pentimento-y way. Or who knows? Maybe you and he will feel as if you each have a perfect marble in your pocket. A beautiful secret tiger-eye marble. No one else will know you have it, but you two will always know it's there."

"A marble?" I made a face. It's not as if I yearn for a marble every time I reach in my pocket. Maybe Matt does. Or Michelangelo did?

"Okay, forget the marble metaphor," Mom said. "You know what the Spanish say?" I shook my head. "*No te pueden quitar lo bailado*" (No Tay Pway Den Key Tar Low Bye La Dough).

"Which means—?"

"Literally: 'If you've gone dancing, no one can take that away from you,'" Mom said. "But loosely: 'You can't take away someone's happy memories.'" I was petting Hedgehog, and Mom added, "You know Comey, my old stuffed animal?"

"The black cat with the green eyes. On my bookshelf." Poor Comey is so so so old that even if you pet her gently, she sheds more than a real cat.

"I don't cuddle Comey anymore," Mom said, "but I like knowing she's there."

"I'll always know where Hedgehog is, even when I'm a grown-up."

"We'll take good care of her," Mom agreed.

"But what do you mean? That you like knowing Antonio is there?"

"Maybe," Mom confessed. "But what's important isn't even so much the Antonio of today, who is in Spain, but the Antonio of years ago. That one is safe and sound within me, like my grandparents and my childhood friends and my college roommates and little ol' Comey. They're part of the person I became, just as this trip is part of who you are—and of who you are becoming." Mom sat up a little straighter as if she suddenly remembered I was her daughter, not some student or grown-up friend. "Melanie, I'm glad I dated Antonio, but I'm glad I *married* Daddy. What I have with Antonio are memories. You know what I have with your daddy?"

"What?"

"Something much better! Not only do Daddy and I have memories, we have the here and now—and we also have two lovely children."

"I wouldn't exactly call Matt the Brat a lovely child."

"Well, I wouldn't trade Matt or Daddy or you for anything or anyone in the world."

"The Old World or the New World?"

"Either," Mom said. "Daddy is the love of my life—he's the one I'm spending my life with."

"What about us?"

"You too! You better believe it!" Mom stood up and got out her airline toothbrush. "And now, young lady, are you ready to go to sleep?"

"Almost almost," I said, "but I still have to write in my diary."

And now, whew, I have!

Hugs and Kisses,
Melanie

P.S.

The present
is
a present,
but memories
make you
who you are.

March 29 morning

Dear Diary,

This time we really are heading home.

Out the window I saw green mountains, brown valleys, and plains polka-dotted with trees. Now all I can see is water water water.

Mom said it's okay that we'll be jet-lagged because we'll feel like going to bed early and waking up early, and that will help us get back on school schedule.

Dad said he can't believe we scored four round-trip international tickets.

"Let's go on another trip this summer!" Matt said.

"Spain again?" I suggested. My brain keeps going over the airport *adiós*. I even like how Spaniards do the ***adiós*** *adiós* *adiós* fade-out thing on the phone because it seems gentler than a regular goodbye.

"What do you think, Marc?" Mom asked. "The kids really enjoyed this trip, and it's been great for Mel's Spanish. Next time we could fly to a beach or to Salamanca or Santiago de Compostela—"

"Not Spain again," Dad said. "I just look *loco*, Me Ron Dah."

"How about London? Or Paris?" I said.

"Maybe," Mom said. "Or as the French say, *peut-être*" (Put Tet Tra).

Dad leaned over and kissed Mom. "You are such a show-off," he teased in the proudest way.

"When do we get home?" Matt asked. "I can't wait to see DogDog."

"Just DogDog?" I said. "What about Lily?"

"Her too," Matt admitted with a dopey smile.

Matt's lucky. So am I. Here's what I believe: My heart does not have corners—it's a great big mosaic. And one of its little pieces will always be a Miguel piece. Maybe more than one!

Even though I don't know when I'll see Miguel again, I like knowing where I can find him: in Spain and in my memory and in my heart.

I also like that my first kiss was with him.

Dad just told me to drink my milk. I said, "How come you don't have to drink *your* milk?" He said he's grown, but I'm *growing*.

Which must be true. (Either that or my closet shrinks my clothes.)

Growing up is okay. But it's weird to be aware of yourself doing it.

Sometimes I think I'm just now starting to figure out life. It's not bulls versus bullies, or good news versus bad news, or true love versus false love, or kids versus adults. It's way more complicated, which, I guess, keeps everything interesting.

Too bad there's no Grandpa Guy to personally explain it all! But even if there were, I would still want to think for myself.

I hope I can keep learning to enjoy things more and worry about them less. I'm trying—but I'm worried it won't be easy!

Wow. I can't believe I'm almost at the end of this new diary. When we get home, I'll put it on my shelf next to my Italy and Holland diaries.

It's strange: I like writing because I like to describe the world from my own point of view. I like reading for the opposite reason—I like to see the world from someone else's point of view.

As for this diary, I bet I'll take it down from time to time, just to reread certain pages. . . .

I am now going to close my eyes and imagine getting an e-mail. An e-mail that's funny and sweet and has a mistake or two. An e-mail that might be signed: *With Love from Spain, Miguel Ramón*.

With Love from the Plane,

Melanie Martin

Olé Olé Olé

to:

My beloved family, or *familia* (Fa Meal E Ah), especially Emme, Elizabeth, and Robert Ackerman; Marybeth, Mark, and David Weston; the Squam Lake cousins; and Mathilde Reategui. They do funny things I get to write about, and they critique my books before they're fully baked.

My friends, or *amigos* (Ah Me Goes), who ask questions, read early drafts, and usually laugh at all the right places: the Wilcox family, Maureen and Arianna Davison, the Gidumals, David Nickoll, and (it's a *tradición*) Olivia Westbrook-Gold.

The Spaniards who have made such a difference: Juan, Mari Carmen, Miriam, Pipo, Gloria, Andreu, Teresa, Roger, Ana, Maru, and Javier Muñoz-Basols.

The remarkable Knopf team, starring Michelle Frey, Sarah Hokanson, Joan Slattery, Kathy Dunn, Michele Burke, Colleen Fellingham, and Marci Roth.

The wonderful Curtis Brown crew, especially Laura Peterson, Kelly Going, Dave Barbor, and Ed Wintle.

Star students Christina Chinloy, Sophie Raseman, Mathilda McGee-Tubb, Stephanie Jenkins, Louisa Strauss, Nina Rose, and all the great kids I've met in classrooms everywhere.

Carol Weston majored in Spanish and French comparative literature at Yale, then met her husband in Madrid, Spain, while earning her master's in Spanish from Middlebury. Today they live in Manhattan with their two daughters. Carol is the "Dear Carol" advice columnist at *Girls' Life* magazine and the author of *The Diary of Melanie Martin; Melanie Martin Goes Dutch; Girltalk: All the Stuff Your Sister Never Told You; For Teens Only; For Girls Only;* and *Private and Personal. With Love from Spain, Melanie Martin* is Carol Weston's tenth book. She has appeared on *The Today Show, The View, Oprah, Montel, 48 Hours*, and other television shows, and her books have been published in Italian, Russian, Czech, Polish, German, Cantonese, Mandarin, and other languages.

You can visit Carol at melaniemartin.com.